I0785208

# ROSE DIAMOND

## RONALD

**Copyright © Issac Brooks 2022**
All rights reserved.

No part of this book may be used or reproduced by any means, graphic, electronic, or mechanical, including photocopying, recording, taping or by any information storage retrieval system without the author's written permission except in the case of brief quotations embodied in critical articles and reviews.

Self-published by
Issac Brooks

Because of the dynamic nature of the Internet, any web addresses or links contained in this book may have changed since publication and may no longer be valid. The views expressed in this work are solely those of the author and do not necessarily reflect the views of the publisher or platform they are published on or through. The author bears sole responsibility for said views.

This book's information, ideas, and suggestions are not intended as a substitute for professional advice. Before following any suggestions in this book, you should consult your financial assistant or firms related to this subject matter. Neither the author nor the publisher shall be liable or responsible for any loss or damage allegedly arising as a consequence of your use or application of any information or suggestions in this book.

# ROSE DIAMOND

## RONALD

ISSAC BROOKS

# PROLOGUE

**A**ll I could hear was my own bartered breathing as the Darkness encased me. Despite how depressing my situation is, I can't deny that for a moment, I still entertained a slither of hope that I could escape. It was the calm that deluded me. A calm that was so short-lived in the beginning of my descent into insanity that it tricked my brain into overdrive. All the while, my body refused to follow the instructions that my overclocked mind managed to relay to it. It wasn't because my body could no longer move. It was because I had become too weak in body and mind to see my thoughts into action. The flesh that I still had left was rotting quickly and barely clung to my bones. The humid air surrounding me only deepened my despair, I could feel any and all sensation I had left on my weak body waning with the passage of time. Soon I would become a husk with no semblance of mortality to it, nothing more than another rotting corpse beneath the earth. My hands and legs were stiff as blocks, but somehow, I managed to move them in my desperate attempts at reprise. Though they probably weigh a million pounds at this point, I managed to lift them in a singular, determined motion. Clawing at the wood.

Regardless of my despair, I still cling to the ghost of sensation that lingers in my cold undying heart. What I feel is the most bitter of all of humanity's poisons. Desperation, fear, regret, sadness… I feel it all in a wicked cocktail of the worst emotions known to man as I continue to claw desperately at the walls of my confine. There is no end to my suffering. I want to believe that the light of day will someday shine on my wretched face so long as I refuse to yield to my grim reality. I want to truly believe that there is hope for me yet, but I have been a fool for far too long. A greater part of me had long broken. It knows that my struggles are pointless and vain- but I resist still. I continue at my dying pace, moving my hands in front of me like I had a chance at clawing away the darkness. This is probably my way of fighting back the constant fear that I am drowning in. But no matter how hard I fight, It feels like I am clawing away at infinity. The darkness will not yield to me; there is no hope. The place where I have been forced to rest is one where hope comes to die and yet I fight still. I am no nobleman. I want to scream, I tried to scream… but I had lost my voice along with my tongue hours ago. Despite knowing fully well that it will be better for me to conserve my air, my desperation had long since replaced my sanity. Any ember of humanity I still clung too had been lost in time.

When I wasn't struggling a futile struggle, I was trying to catch my breath. Breathing was just as futile as escape. A horrible stench filled the air driving away the almost nonexistent oxygen I had left. I found myself gasping for air like fish out of water when there was none to breath nor enough to fill my rotting lungs to the point where I would feel less distraught. When I succumb to despair, the grim reality will set in. The stench of decomposing flesh filled my small coffin and choked me; the stench of my own flesh appalls me. At a certain point in a man's life where he is dying of oxygen deprivation and heaving to the smell of his own flesh, one starts to think; Do I truly deserve this? Given I'm not exactly a nice person, one could even consider me a villain. I am no saint but such torment- NO! I do not deserve this; no one could ever deserve the horror I am forced to endure. To be lost to time, I refused to succumb to despair but deep down, I knew there was no hope for me where I laid. Wherever it was, I laid.

Eventually, I barely had the strength left in me to struggle. Time seemed to have lost all meaning. Whether it was night or day, I would never be able to tell. Darkness. All that was left as darkness. It was too dark for me to see my hands even when I struggled to hold out my hands in front of me, but I could barely feel my fingers, what was left of them at least. The nails on the fingers I had left, had fallen off ages ago along with the skin around it, the cancer had taken most of my flesh and I had scratched what was left of them down to the bones of my fingertips. I finally laid silent in the dark devoid of all hope, helpless; this was how I had remained for a hundred days and nights, crying when I felt hungry and dry but never dying. Hunger and thirst had become a norm but the release I sought would never come. Death would not visit me; I was a damned man. No matter how much I yearned for it, I would not die. I thought back at my life, as shambled and petty as it was- I would trade this hell for it any day. For at this moment, time and death were no longer enemies.

It would always be better than this living hell I now endure. Looking back to my life before this, I had a job, a home, and a family… it wasn't much but it was enough. I see that now. I was never a good man; there's no point lying to myself. I did things that even I found appalling. I neglected my family… 'oh! Helen'

Her name came to mind, but it had been so long. It sounded so foreign and even more so to my barely functioning lips and vocal cords. I could no longer put a face to the name in my head. It's all a blur now. She used to be my wife. I used to be her world at some point, but I neglected the love she had for me until there was nothing left. Now she was somewhere better, I hoped, 'All I ever did was take…take! Take!! I want another wish!' I could barely even speak but I managed to force a semblance of the words out of my mouth. "You can hear me… I know you can. Give me another wish!"

I know he can hear me. I know because I can hear laughing from the depths of the void.

# CHAPTER

## ONE

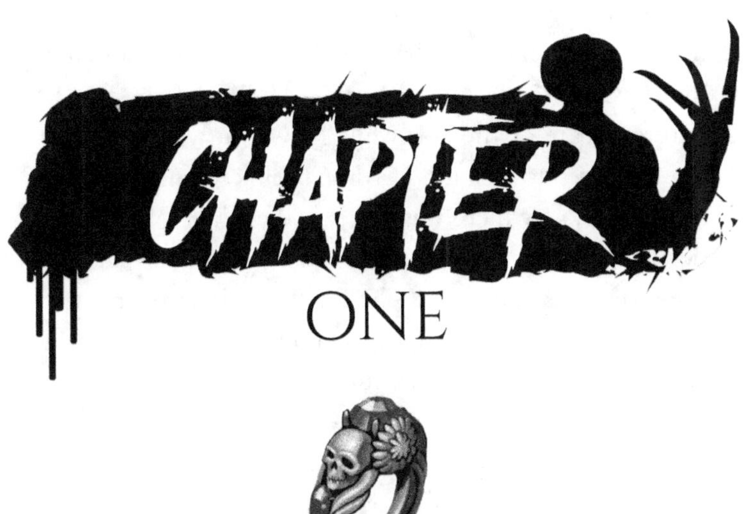

It was a warm Friday morning. Roland Butler had gotten out of bed at 7:15am with the grace of a mindless drone. As always, he did a little stretch in front of the window when he turned and glanced at his wife. Roland was careful not to stir her as he stepped into the bathroom to prepare for the day ahead of him. He had a morning ritual. Every morning he would brush, shave, take an ice-cold shower and then return to find his work clothes ironed neatly on the chair beside his bed. Helen, his wife was still fast asleep at the time, but he was relieved that she at least ensured his clothes were ready for him every day. If she ever decided not to do so, it would simply set Roland up to a bad start. Roland didn't complain, he wasn't going to wake her up over and the issue he felt ignoring would suffice. Helen was out late again. He wasn't up when she got back but he knew for a fact that she must have snuck into bed early that morning after setting his clothes for him; she must have had 'Fun' with her outing. Not that it mattered to Roland, so long as she had his clothes ready and took care of the kids while he was at work, nothing else mattered to Roland. He didn't think too much about it. Roland knew there was more to the whole picture but decided keeping things simple was less tasking. He got dressed and stepped out silently, the kids were in their rooms; he didn't bother to check though. His boys, Gerald and Mark were 7 but they could be quite the handful. He never did check on them on his way out because he always felt he wouldn't make it to work on time if he bothered. He found solace in this monotonous routine. In his garage sat the only thing he loved more than himself. It was a black 2017 Honda Accord he had gotten half-price a year ago. He owned a Honda that he was proud of, but hearing it purr to the life, he frowned. There was something wrong with the engine; he could hear it. Roland just hoped it wasn't anything too serious cause he didn't have the cash to fix it up any time soon. But life's a bitch, it seems.

Tilton Trading Firms. A titan of industries with branches all over North America. There wasn't much to say about the company other than the fact that its pay was good and the work hours seemed convenient. Roland was an Accountant at the branch in his town and despite all the prestige many would expect from such a well-known establishment, Roland hated every moment of working there; from the cheap coffee to the other employees to the boring work he always had to do although he did it well enough to earn a promotion. But nothing did he hate more than his boss, Nicolai Wallace, who seemed to go well out of his way to make life a living hell for Roland. Roland at least found it more bearable, thanks to his routine. Though Nicolai was always holding him back to work longer hours, giving him extra work that was not even part of his docket and always berating him at the drop of a hat. Nicolai was such a pain in the ass that Roland had many times considered quitting. How he longed to flick the chubby son-of-a-bitch off while he waltzed out of the gloomy building with his middle fingers in the air and a rap song in the background, never to return again. Alas, he could only do so in his fantasies.

Roland needed the job and God forbid that his wife ever learnt that he had decided to quit, she would literally blow her top and he would never hear the last of it. It had become a part of their dynamic. He brought the money home and Helen remained a good wife. Roland got to work as early as he always did; he had a spot reserved in the parking lot- the only perk he actually enjoyed from his promotion- and it made his routine all the merrier as he got into the office and greeted his co-workers as he always did, grabbed his coffee as alas did and then walked the familiar path to his own office where he could get to work like a decent human being. But as Roland was on his way to his desk, he noticed something odd. He could have sworn everyone in the office had their eyes on him for some reason, but more so, they had looks of pity while others hard sneering and gloating looks on their annoying ass faces. Roland could almost feel their gazes boring into the back of his head as he glanced nervously at his wristwatch, 8:00am on the dot, so he couldn't have been late he thought back to his last time at work, wondering if he forgot something important. Other than his overly self-conscious sense of awareness that morning, nothing seemed to be put out of place. It must have all been in his head. He shook his head lightly, 'I must be overthinking it' Roland thought reassuringly to himself as he got in his office and shut the door behind him. He let out a sigh of relief and put his briefcase down to get his laptop and the work he had taken home with him. There was a meeting he had to attend in an hour and so he wanted to use all the time he had left to ensure his presentation was in order.

Right before he could get started, barely a minute didn't go by before his door swung open again and there in the wake of the intrusion stood Donald Sutton, the intern. Donald was a tall Texan man with a well-trimmed yet over oiled beard and a pointy nose and an annoyingly charming southern accent. He had started at the main office a few months ago and had become the Boss' favorite lackey, but that only made Roland to hate him. Watching everyone fawn over the young man while all he did was run around getting coffees and kissing ass; although Roland will admit he kisses ass like it were an Olympic skill. Roland scowled at Donald as he cleared his throat and adjusted his glasses for a moment. "Good morning Mr. Butler," Donald greeted, he sounded short of breath, like he had been running and though he tried to look calm, his dark eyes betrayed him, looking worried behind his frames.

Roland didn't respond at first and then Donald gulped breathing in short breaths trying to cover his nervousness. It wasn't a good sign and Roland already had a wide guess as he pinched the base of his nose with a sigh. "He's calling me, isn't he?" Roland murmured while giving a loud and drawn-out exhale.

Of course, Nicolai wouldn't kick his morning off properly without taking a bite out of his least favorite employee. As annoying as it was to admit, that had become part of the bastard's own little routine. 'Let's get this over with,' Roland thought as Donald frowned and watched mutely, as he began to gather any and all the documents and reports he felt his boss might try to berate him about and just then, Donald finally spoke. "You're not going to need any of that?"

"Why not?" Roland asked, puzzled by the intern's remark, which turned out to be a very redundant thing to ask. His answer was just around the corner with a spring in its step.

"Roland! What the hell are you doing in my office?" Nicolai's voice barked long before his face made an appearance at Roland's doorway behind Donald. His boss had a smug look on his fat face and short stature. He reminded Roland of an 80s mafia villain who probably had Salvatore for a surname and reeked of smoke rather than cheap cologne. He asked as he stepped into the office. "Didn't you get my memo?"

"What? I didn't-"

"Of course, you didn't," Nicolai interrupted with a sneer, "Pack your shit and get the fuck out of my office, you incompetent piece of shit!"

Roland was flabbergasted, trying to understand the words that individually were easy to comprehend but were past his current understanding as a whole. Nicolai was an ass, but this was by far the worse he had ever been and what troubled Roland the most was that he was smiling for once. "You can't be serious,"

"Oooh, but I am… You're fired, Roland. Now get the fuck on out of here before I call security." Donald smirked as he tossed a letter on the table and turned to leave proud as a peacock.

Roland stared at the paper in shock. He was in a daze, 'this couldn't be happening'. Roland paled as his gaze went from the letter to Nicolai in the hallway; a bitterness swelled up inside him, followed by a bout of anger as the realization set in as he stood there in disbelief, more anger brimmed from the depth of his heart. He had tolerated so much; this was the very last straw for him, and he could feel that his heart could no longer contain the rage inside of him. "No, you can't be serious. You can't do this to me- Nicolai, get the fuck back here! You can't do this to me!" Roland snapped as he followed after Nicolai. The air was still with tension and the office was deadly silent as everyone watched quietly with the silence of owls in flight. Nicolai paused on his stubby legs from his confident and victorious gait and stared bewilderedly back at Roland. He looked as though he were staring at a pig with wings. Roland couldn't believe that he had actually said that out loud. He could feel everyone else in the building staring at him as though he had lost his mind, but he had summoned the courage to call Nicolai out, so he was going speak regardless. "9 years… I've been here 9 years. That's 9 years of working my ass off with your assholes! So much for 9 years of me having your back and putting up with our shit and you're just going to fire me with no reason?"

"No reason...Oooh! I got the reason," Nicolai glared, "That your gloomy face is reason enough. Don't even get me started on your unruly conduct and antisocial tendencies that are more hazardous to the work environment and the well-being of the staff around you, that scam you tried to pull was the final straw. Now get the fuck out-"

"I call bullshit!" Roland snapped; he wasn't just going to stand there and listen to all the garbage Nicolai was spewing.

Scam? What scam! Roland gaped at the man pointing fingers at him to justify unlawfully laying him off. He knew very well that Nicolai was referring to an accounting error that he had failed to report about a month ago, but that couldn't be the reason for his sanction because he handled it. He already had the account balanced with a cut from his salary and in all his years, he had done his very best to maintain a healthy work mentality. Sure, Roland was distant, but he always interacted with his fellow staff and aided the others when they requested it even though he hated all of them, but this is America, a very hypocritical nation. Despite the obvious truth that he was not fond of being bothered at work, he was very approachable. The bastard simply wanted him gone. There was nothing Nicolai could say to convince him otherwise. Roland was speechless and Nicolai smirked. A smirk that only irritated Roland even more.

"Cat got your tongue?" Nicolai smirked as Roland fumed with rage, his fists balled. He always knew that Nicolai would try and screw him over someday. He didn't expect that everyone else present would simply stand by without standing up for it and watch it all happen like they were ignorant sheep. He glanced about the office, glaring at everyone watching. 'What's this? What are you all staring at?' it infuriated Roland that his misfortune had become some sort of display for all of them. Roland was filled with nothing but disdain as he turned and returned to get his briefcase while Donald stood in the center office with a look as though he were lost and confused. Nicolai had a smug look on his face. One Roland wished he could knock right off his face. He must have felt victorious or at least he did before Roland returned and sent him railing into a water dispenser with a fist to the face, blotting out his right eye.

"You can keep your fucking job," Roland spat as he left his boss rocked, soaked, embarrassed and fuming behind him. 'I was going to quit soon anyway.'

Roland wanted to find content in knowing that he had gotten the last laugh or rather last hit but there was no laugh. Yes, he had finally given Nicolai a piece of his mind but now he was out of a job with his right fist throbbing like hell from his ill-thrown punch and now there he was in his car, slamming his palm on the steering wheel of his car like a man on a mental break. Roland wanted to leave. It didn't matter where he went so long as he was far away from the damn Tilton building or anything that would remind him of it, in fact. His car's engine sputtered to life as he squeezed the steering wheel tightly and gritted his teeth. "Fuck! Fuck!" He cursed in a fit as he slammed his balled fist into the steering wheel over and over again.

'What now?' Roland glared at his reflection. He had just burnt a bridge and now not only was there no going back, knowing how much Nicolai despised him, but he was also almost certain of getting handed a lawsuit or something for assault. He drove out of the building's parking lot distraught; getting laid off was just one of the things eating at his mind. He remembered the look everyone gave him on his way out; even before he'd stepped out, he could hear them whispering about him. It could have been anybody... what happened to him could have happened to anyone else, he hissed. He didn't want to think about them anymore; he never liked any of them, to begin with. It didn't matter if they were talking behind his back or to his face; what mattered to Roland was thinking of how to break the news to his wife and kids and more importantly, what to do next. Cause lord knows he will not be getting a glowing letter of recommendation; he'll be lucky not to be blacklisted. He stopped at a red light; soon as he did, he buried his face in his palms and audibly sighed. Thinking about his family didn't help to reduce his worries; it annoyed him instead. Roland was sure having to deal with his wife and kids getting on him about money and just the thought of it is already unbearable. Barely an hour had gone by and yet he had become a mess. He was at a junction. He didn't even know how he got there with the messy thoughts in his head. A straight path would have taken him home, while a quick turn to the right would lead him right to his favorite bar. Well, at this point, it's a no-brainer, he thought. He tapped his fingers on the steering wheel and calmed himself with deep breathes, 'Never too early for a drink,' he thought as he began to turn the wheel. Life couldn't get any worse was the last thought in his mind when his engine died.

"No, this can't be happening to me," Roland gasped as he struggled with his key. It didn't matter how hard he tried; his car would purr and sputter and still not come on. A blaring horn jeered him as he glanced at his rearview mirror to find a man in a pickup truck impatiently blasting his horn at him, successfully bringing Roland out of his dazed state. Roland just realized the streetlights were green, signaling him to go and he was in the way. "No, this can't be fucking real!"

He keyed the engine again and muttered under his breath as the truck swerved by him with the driver's friend in the front seat, giving him the middle finger. "Asshole!" The man jeered at Roland as Roland in turned glared daggers back at them. Today just wasn't his day.

"Go fucking die!" Roland retorted at them in a fit; honestly, he wished they would just up and die. Then for the first time all morning, Roland had gotten something he wished for. It was like a scene out of a horror movie, the noise in the surrounding scene suddenly becoming distant save for the pickup truck, its incoming co-victim. Everything seemed to move in slow motion to Roland; that way, he saw it all unfold. A trailer had lost control of its brakes and slammed right into the side of the truck he was yelling at just seconds after it drove past the traffic light. There was a moment of silence where Roland was shaken to his bones by shock. He was speechless as he saw a hand that had flicked him off get flung across the street, leaving a trail of blood, while the men he saw just seconds ago were crushed so badly he couldn't tell where the car started and they ended. It was all a giant metallic mush of scrap metal and gore; he couldn't even tell where the trailer and the pickup met. Both vehicles seemed to have fused together in the most violent way imaginable. Roland heard someone scream and a crowd began to form at the accident scene. He was petrified, clinging to his steering wheel in one hand while the other hand was still keying the engine, all the while shaking like a lost child on the winter solstice. Then in the spirit of things finally going his way, the familiar sputter, his car coming back to life, the sound of the engine was what snapped him out of the trance-like state he had entered.

Roland gulped with a heavy heart as he drove past the crash. If getting fired wasn't enough, the horrendous sight of mangled corpses was something he needed a drink to get out of his head. Especially because, although stupid, the thought that all this was his fault couldn't escape his wondering thoughts.

# CHAPTER
## TWO

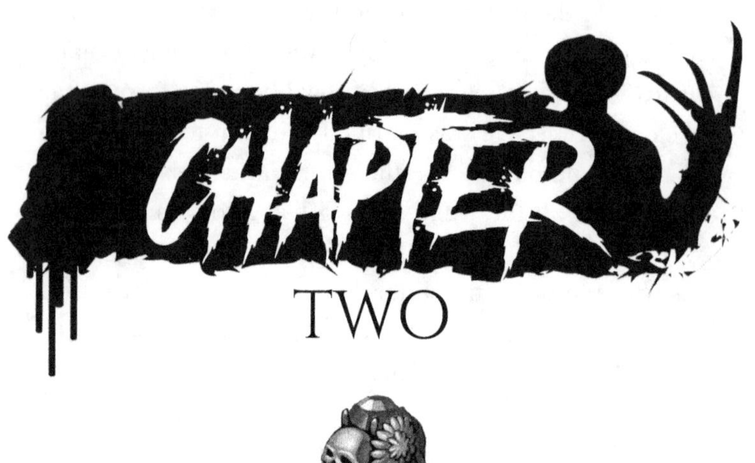

Do they say horror is just as inescapable as death or is it death is an inescapable horror? It makes you wonder what really counts as horror because seeing is way worse than watching such a thing in the cinemas. For Roland, horror was defined by the movies he saw and all the stories he'd heard growing up. He wasn't fond of scary stories, but he'd listened to a bunch of them anyway, 'Fucking campfires,' he thought. He wanted to believe it would take a lot to unnerve or scare him. Today was an exception; Roland had never seen a person die before, more so after he said they should do so at that. Sure, he'd seen a body at a funeral or two, but this was the first time he had ever seen a human being be reduced to nothing more than a soulless paste. It made him grim with fear, 'That could have been me,' He thought as he strolled over to a bench at the Bar's counter and mounted himself there. The Bartender knew Roland and could tell from the look on his face that he was shocked or something. He didn't ask what Roland wanted. He took a wild guess and gave Roland his usual. A gin on ice but filled up the cup this time. The only time Roland snapped out of his trance was when he downed the contents of the glass placed in front of him with a request for another. He couldn't get the image of the accident out of his head, not until his 5th glass when someone uninvited took the seat beside him. Roland didn't really care about anything that wasn't either in his glass or going to make him feel less shitty than he already did.

"I'll have whatever he's having. It looks a hell of a lot better than what I usually have." The stranger of a man cheered. Roland didn't so much as glance at him; the man had a good voice, Roland noticed but he was far from a good enough mood to socialize. He felt the man was trying to approach him or something, but he ignored him. 'Whatever he had to sell' Roland thought, "I'm not buying."

"Who said I was going to sell it to you?" The man snickered as their drinks arrived.

Roland hadn't realized his thoughts were starting to roll off his tongue; he shrugged and took another drink. Halfway down, he paused and grimaced. He'd reach that point where he was more liquor than logic and even the little voice in his head was starting to slur. He decided to pace himself, remembering that heading home drunk was the last thing he wanted to do, or there was nothing worse than a jobless deadbeat drunk. While he was lost in thought, the small flat screen hanging over the bar's counter drew his attention with the new channel's opening theme. The accident was on the news, 'So much for getting it out of my system,' he thought dejectedly.

Roland gagged and forced the bile that tried to rise up from the pits of his stomach at the sight of the crash back down with what was left of his drink. That managed to stop him, but it also caused the man he was trying to ignore to notice him. Roland was starting to feel he'd had a few too many, but that didn't stop him from finishing his drink anyway.

"Ghastly accident, wasn't it." He started.

Roland glanced at the man. He was finally noticing the features other than his voice. Strange was the only way to describe the man he was staring at, and it wasn't just because of how he approached him. The man's eyes were odd, He spoke with an accent that Roland couldn't quite discern, and he dressed awfully flashy for someone in a low-bit bar downtown. The strangest thing about the man though were his eyes. One was a darkish red and the other a bright blue. It must have been some sort of genetic disorder or something- Roland had heard about the condition before. Heterochromia iridis was what the disorder was called if he remembered correctly. It was rare and was what intrigued Roland the most about the man. The man smiled when Roland realized he was staring.

"If you think that's ghastly, you should have seen it for yourself," Roland grimaced.

"Dreadful thing…" The man sighed, "Such a sight would make you feel as though you were next, although that's not the way I'll want to go."

Roland swallowed loudly. The man was right; he had thought so, too and as he drank, he wanted nothing more than to forget that horrid sensation of being stalked by death like it was telling him to count the days. Roland scowled at the man. "What do you want?" He glared, "Cause if it's cash, I ain't got any to spare."

"I don't want your money and I ain't got anything to sell you either," The man laughed over his drink as he gestured to the waiter and got Roland another drink. Roland eyed the man suspiciously but didn't refuse the drink. He had just lost his job; he was going to accept all the free stuff he could get. "On the contrary, I felt you'd like some company… you look like you're down on your luck and I'm nothing if not charitable."

Roland scowled at the fluid in his glass. For a moment, his thoughts had strayed, and he began to wonder how easily a little colored liquid could make his problems disappear, only to come back whenever later

"…Together with liver issues," he mused silently and then he acknowledged the stranger again with a spry laugh. "I'm married, buster although as I say this, I'm starting to think it won't last, and even if I weren't, I don't swing that way."

The man laughed. "You're a funny one."

Oddly Roland didn't mind. The man knew how to talk, Roland could admit that and when the strange man bought him a few more drinks, he had a way to make Roland open up; it wasn't long before he was ranting about work and how very obvious his wife's affair was. Roland couldn't tell why he felt so inclined to open up to the man. He told him all the things he has been bottling up, which felt good and therapeutic even, but as he did it, he felt as though they were the only two present in the bar. Even when the place got crowded with its regulars and very much wasn't, that fact still wasn't enough to burst the little bubble they made or enough to disrupt their conversation.

"That sounds like a lot for one man," The man scowled as he slammed his empty cup on the counter,

"It is a lot for one man," Roland agreed as he snapped over what could have been his 8th glass, but he had lost count. Talking to the stranger made it difficult for him to get drunk. In fact, despite how much he had drunk, Roland was still sober enough to think clearly and strangely enough, he might be able to drive. "But that's the thing, I ain't like most men. I'm resourceful, and strong, and-"

"Lucky..." The stranger chipped into Roland's confusion, "If you weren't, it would have been you in the crash earlier."

"Yeah... you're right," Roland mused; he had almost forgotten about the crash he witnessed and didn't feel as sickened at the thought of it as he did earlier that morning. "Although...' he mused as he stared down his glass before looking up, "or I can put it to the universes as a way of not kicking me when I'm down."

Again, he glanced at the bottom of the glass in his hand and scowled. It was uncharacteristic of him to open up so much, especially to a random man at the bar- He blamed the booze. "I think I've had too much to drink," Roland finally admitted.

"Nonsense!" The man cheered gutsily, "I can barely feel a buzz coming on and I feel you need a little more- Waiter, get us two more glasses on me."

"Nah… Awfully generous and all," Roland interjected as he got up to surprisingly steady feet and reached for his wallet, "It's getting late; my wife's probably worried sick."

The stranger smiled and offered to pay, which Roland gratefully accepted as he really needed cash at this point which now that he that he thought about it as a bad idea to have come to a bar in the first place, He just sighed but as Roland tried to leave the man held Roland's hand with a firm grip for someone dressing so flamboyant. Roland was baffled by how cold the man's touch felt and stared back at the man in confusion, wondering if there were even close enough to be hand-holding. The man asked. "Are you a believer, Roland?"

Roland stared quizzically at the man before letting out a chuckle.

"Is that what this was all about? You all are using liquor to evangelize now?" He laughed, thinking about how low religion has fallen but the strange man was deadly serious. He could tell from the intensity behind his contrasting gaze.

"Not in God, silly." The strange man replied, "Something greater than that the one above all, if you will."

Roland was hesitant but sat back down for a moment. He wasn't entirely eager to go home just yet, so this line of thought was really intriguing to him and considering that the stranger was paying for his drinks, he figured it was best he left things on a good note. "I'm not exactly a

Christian, nor do I even generally like them, but I don't believe you should be saying shit like that so openly."

The strange man smirked.

"I thought you were the kind of man who didn't care what crap the people around you would spout," The strange man said, and Roland laughed.

"Well, you have me there, but there are stupid things to say and there's that…" He admitted, "But if you want a decent life, you're gonna have to conform to what 'These people' consider the norm or its fire and brimstone, my man."

"Well… what if I told you there was a way to get everything you wanted easy and risk-free, without giving a shit about the norm and what others would think?" The strange man propositioned and though Roland wanted to believe he wasn't interested, the man's words had got his attention- hook, line, and sinker.

"I'm listening," Roland replied as the man took a small case out from his large coat's inner pocket. The case the stranger held before him was black, probably made out of velvet, so Roland could already tell that whatever was inside it must have been just as high quality as the case it came in; the man opened the case and revealed a ring to him. The ring was a sight to behold and yet held an eerie aesthetic to it. The ring itself was the kind that had a way to make a person stare at it for hours on end. It was a black overall ring with two eye-catching black skulls along its rig with three red diamonds spaced out on the top of it and along its sides. "This beauty right here… is the Rose Diamond Ring."

"Wow… fascinating," Roland gasped; he wasn't a fan of jewelry aside from the occasional Rolex but once he laid eyes on the ring, he couldn't seem to take his eyes off them. They were enchanting so much that one can get lost in looking at them or rather staring, in fact, Roland found himself unconsciously reaching out for it before he reined himself in at the thought of a price. He was more than certain that he wouldn't be able to afford such a thing he wondered if he could even afford the box. "That's a lovely ring and all, but sadly I can't afford it."

"It's free…" The strange man laughed,

"Nothing is free," Roland immediately replied, "You see, Roland, This ring is made of magic hell, it basically is magic and grants the wearer, which will soon be your three wishes when you wear it. All you've got to do is ask and believe."

"A gem like this… doesn't look cheap nor free either," Roland raised a brow at the man. He wasn't even concerned with the part where a stranger was insisting some piece of jewelry could grant wishes. Roland felt he would have been satisfied with the ring as it was. But with a ring of this quality, he was starting to ask what was wrong with the head of the one who gave it away.

"Believe… Roland. All you have to do is wish and believe," The man insisted, "I'd tell the finer details some other time since you seem to be in a hurry,"

Roland was very skeptical about the whole transaction and eyed the case he now held curiously as the man left the bar. Like a switch, Roland snapped back to reality. It was 5:30 in the evening and he was holding unto a ring from a man whose name he never bothered to ask. "Hey!

You forgot-" Roland snapped as he darted out after the man to find that he was gone. "You forgot your ring,"

He hesitated outside the bar for a moment before he stuffed the ring in his pocket. Nothing else was keeping him at the bar, the man had paid for all the drinks and so he decided it was about time he went home.

# CHAPTER
## THREE

**T**he drive home was an easy one. Roland was still a bit troubled about his day, but somehow he'd managed to bury all that worry beneath the euphoria of his buzz. He was more eager to learn what Helen had whipped up for dinner. When he got home, he saw an odd sight. There was a grey Jeep in the driveway. Roland couldn't help but notice it as he drove into the garage. He assumed it must have been one of his neighbors' but then again, he was almost certain none of them drove one. It seemed a bit much for his dull neighbor's taste and stuck out on his neighborhood block like a sore thumb. "I'm home," He declared groggily as he got inside. He was having a throbbing headache and looked like shit. All he wanted to do was get some water, a hearty meal, and some shut-eye so he could come up with a plan later when he was well-rested and sober. So much time had gone by, and he felt hungover but oddly couldn't remember getting drunk for a second at the bar. Odd, Roland had grown used to having his boys jump him as soon as he walked through the front door, yet they were nowhere to be found, though, in all honesty, he was relieved they spared him that evening. He was almost certain he would have easily toppled over like a hollow trashcan if they did. He heard the kids' laughter coming from the living room. They must have been distracted by something, he thought and so he headed over there to see them, but just before he turned the corner, he heard another voice, one that he couldn't recognize. There was a man in the living room playing with them and when he stepped out, he was met by an unfamiliar face. 'Daddy!' the boys cheered when they saw their father as they rushed over to hug Roland with cheerful smiles, but the man stood there. He was like a deer caught in headlights. "You smell funny, daddy," Gerald scrunched his nose at the scent of alcohol on his dad's breath just before their mom, Helen, walked out of the kitchen.

Helen hesitated in the hallway for a second. She seemed alarmed.

"Daddy's tired go to your room. You've got school tomorrow." Helen cooed to the boys as she pried the kids off their father in an almost panicked state. Roland was absentminded; he was watching the man in the living room with a cold gaze the entire time. The man was younger, probably in his mid-20s and was wearing a vintage shirt with kakis when he nervously tried to greet Roland. He could see the appeal in the youth. However, it was going to take a lot more than appeal to explain what he was doing in Roland's house.

"Sup…" Roland nodded, acknowledging the man as Helen turned to face him. Roland didn't need an explanation; he could already tell who the young man in his living room was supposed to be. After all, Roland knew that Helen barely tried to hide her lover from him but seeing the man in his house gave him mixed up emotions- all of which bordered along the lines of disdain and disgust and a surprising amount of amusement, especially for Helen's daring. Helen had her heart in her throat as she watched the two of them. The pressure in the air felt as though a dam was about to burst and Helen was afraid she and her lover were about to bear the brunt of it all.

"Marcus, why don't you go up and make sure the kids are in bed, huh" Helen finally spoke, breaking the silence as the man, Marcus, she called him, hurried up the stairs behind her like he couldn't get out fast enough. She looked calm enough, but Roland could tell his wife was on edge. Helen then turned to find Roland followed the young man with a glare in his eyes and she immediately tried to explain. "You see; Marcus is a"

"I don't care what Marcus is," Roland growled, "All I do care about is what he's doing in my house."

"He was helping with the kids-"

"Well, I'm gonna help him to the door!" Roland snapped as he forced his way past Helen and was halfway up the stairs before she caught him by the wrist.

"Stop it! Not in front of the kids!" She pleaded and Roland glared back at her.

"Not in front of the kids…" He snapped; the statement felt like a load of bull to his ears. "You're flaunting your boyfriend in front of the very same kids, and you expect me to keep calm? - Don't act like you thought about the kids when you brought that man into my house."

"Oh… don't play that card. Marcus wouldn't be here if you were a real man and owned up to your mistakes. You smell like shit Roland!"

"My mistakes? What mistakes the fuck are you talking about!"

"I don't know; care to tell me about how you got your ass fired?" She retorted, to Roland's surprise.

He wanted to jeer at her, but no words came out of his mouth when he tried to speak. He was literally speechless at the moment. The only thing on his mind was the question, 'How did she know?'

"Your boss called me after you left work," Helen explained, "What the hell did you do? Cause he sounded pissed as hell,"

"I didn't do anything-"

"He sure as hell sounded like you did," Helen scowled with her arms crossed in front of her and Roland palmed his face. He took deep breaths and then he eyed her coldly. Roland could tell what she was doing.

"So, it's my fault your boyfriend is in my house?"

"I guess it is," Helen frowned, "If you weren't so headstrong and incompetent all the time, then maybe-" she tried to be the one in the right.

"Don't fucking lecture me about competence when you run around like a whore behind my back!" Roland snapped as he grabbed her by the shoulders. He had tried his very best to be calm and felt he was being too lenient with her. She squealed as her eyes were filled with genuine fear as she quivered in front of him.

"All you've done is be a pain in my side; I don't need you telling me my worth when you're useless to me! All I've ever done is be by you and provide for you and I guess Marcus is my thanks."

"Bro, chill out!" Marcus called from the top of the stairs.

"Shut the fuck up, kid; the grownups are talking!" Roland growled back at Marcus. He was a wild beast where he stood, looming over Helen.

Roland glared at the young man. Marcus was very easy on the eyes; Roland could see what Helen saw in him. Despite his build, he seemed confident even though he was doing a poor job of masking his nervousness. It took one glance for Roland to know that he wouldn't like Marcus. Roland could tell the man was frightened by him and he had every right to be; Roland was twice his size and was more than certain that if it came to a fight, he could snap the young man like a twig. And yet seeing how genuinely concerned the man was for his wife made him grimace; it was almost as though he was the villain in their love story. Then he noticed Helen was crying softly in his arms.

"Don't fucking cry like this isn't your fault," Roland scowled, "I'm the victim here."

'Why does no one get that!' Roland thought bitterly as he shoved her back into the railing of the staircase and continued down the stairs in a hard march while Marcus rushed to her side like some sort of knight in shining armor, here to save Helen from a loveless marriage.

"Where are you going?" She called to him as Roland snatched his coat from the coat rack by the entrance and knocked it to the ground along with all the other coats on it.

"Don't act like you suddenly care," Roland jeered, "You know Helen. I knew all about your cheating; you should work on your poker face, by the way, but to bring him into our house when you know I'll be home is just another level of messed up shit,"

Helen bowed her head. Was it a shame? Roland didn't seem to care as he continued.

"And keep your boyfriend off my bed, or don't- I don't want to pretend I fucking care anymore! So, you know what; go away with your little lover boy or whatever but you better be so far away from my house when I get back-in fact, take the kids with you."

In his fit, Roland took his Honda and vanished into the night, leaving a worried wife standing in the driveway with her lover nervously trying to console her. Seeing them together felt like salt to his wounds; it made him floor the gas petal so he could get away faster.

THE STREETS WERE ALMOST DESERTED AND SO ROLAND decided to vent his rage by flooring the gas pedal some more. He didn't care if some cop pulled him over or if his brakes decided to give up on him. The neon lights of the night looked like shooting stars zipping past the corner of his eye, but not even that display was enough to quell his rage. Bitter. Roland felt bitter- about his wife, his job, his day… Roland never thought a day would come where he would feel nothing but hate at being alive. His day was a total shit show and if Roland thought the night couldn't get any worse, he was in for a big surprise when his Honda broke down 12 blocks away from home. 'Fuck! Fuck!! Fuck!' He roared furiously as he pounded his fist into the steering wheel until he feared the airbag would burst out and snap his neck or something before he calmed down and broke into tears instead. He wasn't sad about his fight with Helen, nor the fact that he had left his home for another man and of course, not about his job. Roland felt defeated, his pride was wounded and that was eating at him; he started to wonder at the pointlessness of his life. He got out of his car and glanced about the street he was on. He was still wearing his clothes from work, but he had already removed his tie. He recalled absent-mindedly taking it off as he got home and in his fit, he left it in the doorway. Roland grimaced. The streets weren't deserted; on the contrary, it was pretty lively. With all the other nocturnal members of society trying to find their poison as they prowled the streets in skimpy skirts and dark shirts and ridiculous amount of makeup like, don't they know they basically light up under fluorescent lights? He spotted a seedy hotel down the street and decided he would be spending the night there. He didn't have cash but when he paid for the room, he ordered a shit ton of booze from his credit card. Given the shady place, he wondered if they'd send him a hooker.

The room he got was better than he had expected it to be, not that he was expecting much, to begin with. The sign out front had him expecting pretty poor accommodations. The room had a dormant green hue to it, from the sheets to the pillows. There wasn't a TV, not that he had any intention of watching anything. So long as the place had running water, a working AC and didn't smell like piss, he would be satisfied. He threw himself into the bed and sighed. It was hard to the touch and unwelcoming. Roland felt like a brick wall would have cushioned him a lot better than the bed did. Then he glanced at his phone; he had forgotten to get his charger, and it was plugged beside his bed back home. Thinking of home made his mouth bitter; he couldn't help but imagine Helen and her new 'boy toy' Marcus getting freaky. '…In my bed' He fumed at the thought and palmed his face.

"Wait, why did I have to leave, and they stayed." He mused to himself. It was his house; if anyone had to leave, it was Helen and her dumb boyfriend, not him. Now that he thought about it, the whole incident felt like a stupid mistake. Like he was a dog fleeing with its tail between its legs. The whole thing was frustrating. Roland needed a distraction, so he fled to the comfort of his mobile phone. He didn't have any games on his mobile but then he was convinced that simply exploring the internet for memes or skits would at least liven his mood, but he noticed he had two missed calls. 'Huh… I didn't hear it ring' He leered at the device; the calls must have come in while he was occupied or driving. No surprise that neither was from his disloyal wife; they were from Donald. "What does this prick want?" He frowned just as another call from him came in.

Roland hesitated for a moment, a bigger part of him wanted to ignore it but he answered the call anyway, he had his reasons. Knowing Donald, he was the kind that wouldn't stop calling until he did. "The hell do you want?" He growled after the beep.

"Mr. Butler, good evening" Donald started frantically as Roland rolled his eyes.

"Called to gloat?" Roland hissed,

"Heavens no-" Donald tried to protest, but Roland wouldn't give him the chance to explain himself. He was simply bitter and knowing the young man was probably better off than he was filled Roland with envy.

"Then get to the point; the fuck do you want, Donald?" Roland snapped, "Not glad you cleared out my desk?"

"It wasn't my fault, sir. I didn't want you fired; in fact, I pled against it-" Donald insisted,

Ronald found the man's words hard to believe but gritted his teeth and decided to listen when Donald continued.

"I'm so sorry about this morning, and I understand what you're going through. But it's about Mr. Nicolai."

"What about the prick?" Roland sighed exasperatedly.

"He's threatening to sue you for assault," Donald said as Roland shot up the bed with a fire in his eyes.

"That son of a bitch!" Roland jeered, "First, he fired me and now he wants to bury me in debt! The fucks wrong with him"

"I- it ...t's awful. I know that's why I intervened."

"How?"

"He had a proposition. He said he'd drop the case if I got you to apologize…" Donald said, "I know you don't have a reason to and that everything was his fault, but I feel it's in your best interest to."

Roland was too enraged to care for anything else Donald had to say, so he cut the call and smashed his phone against the hotel wall, panting in rage as Donald's words played back in his head. He had had enough bullshit for one day and Nicolai was his tipping point. Roland balled his fists in his hair and crumbled unto his knees in a daze. He was panting. It felt like the walls were caving in on him. Roland was frustrated. 'How am I getting out of this? This shouldn't be happening to me. Why me? What in god's name did I do to deserve this' A myriad of thoughts ran through his mind and just when he thought he was about to lose his shit, there was a knock at his door. 'Room service,' the voice called and almost instantly Roland was back to a semblance of his graceful self as he opened the door and accepted the drinks from the young lady the front desk had sent to him. The drinks were well chilled and though Roland could argue that he had already drank way too much for one day, there was no other way to mend his aching heart than to pour booze down his throat until it burned. He didn't give a shit about anything else anymore, so he said, 'Fuck it!'

IF DEPRESSION HAD A SCENT, THEN ROLAND BUTLER REEKED of it, and if he didn't, then he obviously smelt like a man that had found his way to the bottom of far too many bottles. It was only a matter of time before Roland's room smelt like a brewery. All his concerns about money had gone out the window and the last of his pride had been flushed down the toilet when he took a piss. He might have as well drank the hotel dry. He'd bled his credit card in spite at his wife, just in case she ever thought to run with his money. It didn't matter though. None of that mattered. The world was made of shit and Roland was the only one who could smell just how bad it reeked. He'd drank so much he was seeing double. He threw up, passed out and woke up within the hour to return to another bottle. He could barely even stand at the time, whatever the time was. He couldn't tell how long he'd been drinking or how late it was either, not that any of that mattered anymore. It wasn't like he had work in the morning to worry about. Roland grimaced and laughed. He didn't know how he felt; one thing was for sure though. He was drunk, yet for the first time ever, that didn't seem to help, and he didn't feel any better. Instead, it was almost like the booze was only make his head hurt just as bad as his heart ached. Liquor was Roland's cure to everything. It was liquid confidence most of the times, a pain killer at others and above all a damn good anti-depressant. It was Roland's magic juice.

The magic juice he could always find in a bottle was Roland's go to prescription but that evening, he learnt that his magic juice doesn't apparently work when you hit a particular level of crappy. Roland was stubborn though rather than cry himself to sleep, he concluded that if he wasn't happy, then he hadn't drunk enough just yet. Eventually, he'd had way too much and passed out again. Hours later, Roland woke up feeling less than stellar. It was safe to say he had more alcohol than blood flowing to his brain and his ears were ringing when he rolled over. Roland felt irritated by everything, but that just meant he needed a little more to drink. He knocked a lamp over as he reached for a bottle of gin he had not noticed was already empty when he rolled to the other side of the bed restlessly. He was out of liquor. Roland didn't realize he had drunk it all during his little pity party. 'Shit! It's empty… there's got to be more.' Roland thought groggily as his ears wouldn't stop ringing and he stumbled out of bed. He stood up too quickly and was very disoriented for a moment. Roland hesitated as he regained his balance, just standing in the middle of the room in nothing but his underwear, and when he managed to pull himself together, the first thing he tried to do was check on the lamp he had knocked over. Luckily it was still in one piece, the same couldn't be said about his phone though. He grunted and swore under his breath at the mess he'd made. Roland thought of how upset Helen would have been had she seen it but then he paused and thought to himself, 'She's the reason I'm even in this mess.'

Roland was drunk, frustrated, and bitter when he glanced at his phone. Somehow it had survived his furious onslaught, though it wasn't without a few battle scars. Its screen was in pieces with ink blotting over most of it and its casing was missing but it still worked well enough for him to tell it was ringing. The phone had obviously seen better days.

As drunk as Roland was, he was still very curious to know who it was calling him at such an odd hour of the night. He assumed it was odd cause it was dark out and that was pretty much all he could tell. Usually, he wouldn't be up so late but tonight wasn't a usual weekday night to Roland. It was small but he still clung to a slither of hope at some relief from the horrible day he'd had. He wouldn't admit it, but he wished it was Helen and that he somehow managed to answer the call so she could apologize for being such a whore and beg him to come home and that she'd be a better wife. Roland had a smirk on his face, "Hell yeah…" Roland cheered awkwardly. It was the liquor in his system deluded him but that sure did put a smile on his face before he even took a closer look at what was left of the damn screen to learn the truth. It was very disappointing, to say the least. When he took a closer look at the phone, through his weird squinting, he realized the call was one of many from the last person on earth he wanted to speak to. His boss, Nicolai. Roland grumbled and cursed. He sat back in bed and tossed the phone unto a chair while he palmed his face. A cool breeze blew over him and he shivered. It had taken him far too long to notice how cold it was, and soon as he did, he glanced about the room, eager to find his clothes. When he reached for his clothes in a pile at the corner of the room, he couldn't help but wonder why he had thought stripping to fall asleep was a good idea. Now that he was up, it felt as though he was trying to freeze his ass off. He desperately wanted them back on again.

As he picked his clothes up off the floor, he heard a small thud like something had fallen. It was the case he had gotten from the stranger at the bar; it fell out and popped up conveniently, revealing the jeweled ring held within it.

"Diamond rose..." Roland cooed at the ring. That was the name he remembered the stranger call it. 'Such a peculiar thing,' Roland thought absentmindedly as he went on both his knees beside the ring when he tried to pick it. He treated the ring like an egg, he was honestly afraid it would fall apart for the rest of his life if he manhandled it. Roland chuckled a little for no reason, the ring was lovely and when he thought of the position he was in, he wondered if anyone who saw him would think he was worshipping the ring. 'Of course not...' Roland couldn't tell that his little protest didn't off as more than a thought. He felt someone of his standard was lucky to have even laid his eyes on such a fine piece of jewelry.

'Do you believe...' the words rang through his mind at that moment. Roland thought of the stranger. Such a strange man, Roland laughed as he picked the ring up and twirled his finger about the gems that encrusted it. He felt the skulls were a nice touch; it gave the ring a gothic feel. The ring was heavy, and he liked that; he was aware that usually, gold was heavy, so assumed that the ring being heavy meant it was valuable. He was actually too drunk to care about the minor details. He simply felt compelled to wear the ring regardless. He took his wedding ring and flung it across the room. Roland felt no guilt discarding his ring because to him. Their marriage was already as good as dead. He slid the ring on his index finger and was charmed to learn it fit like a glove like it was made for him. He was admiring the gems on his finger when suddenly, there was this sharp prickling feeling that had him squeezing his palm. The pain was bearable, and he chuckled when he remembered what the strange man had said. "A magic ring."

Roland held his hand overhead and admired his ring. Belief had never looked so simple.

"If I could wish for anything in the world… I'd wish them all away. Fuck it! I wish all those bastards would just fucking die and suffer even. Nicolai, Marcus- and my whore of a wife too! Who cares about the fucking kids- she can have them! Let them all suffer and the last thing in their minds will be the image of me laughing at their plight." Roland growled with a balled fist. He didn't care if the ring was magic or not; speaking his mind gave him bliss. Almost more bliss than the sight of a bottle that wasn't already empty, just lying by the bed that he was only just noticing. "There you are,"

He coughed as he treated himself to more booze and soon as that was done, he crawled back under his bed sheets and slept soundly. He had drunk himself to a stupor and was too intoxicated to tell that one of the bright red gems on his ring had started to fade from blood red till it died and turned into a pitch-black rock.

# CHAPTER
## FOUR

Screams. There was nothing but darkness and the persist screams coming from deep within it. Roland couldn't sleep over all the screaming. He couldn't tell if it was a dream or if someone was truly crying out to him. When there wasn't darkness, he could see the faint outlines of people in a distance. There was a woman and then a man and then children. They were the source of the blood-curdling cries piercing the darkness. Their voices echoed horridly as their screams berated his soul. They were in agony, and their death cries sent shivers down Roland's spine. Their screams were too loud to even make up what they were saying or rather shouting, although once or twice he could barely hear his name or what sounded like it through their deranged cries. Then he heard something other than a scream and at first, he was glad, but then he realized it was laughter.

Someone was laughing at him. The laughter was the eerie kind that sends shivers down your spine. In all that darkness, Roland was forced to face a jarring reality, the reality that he wasn't alone. He darted about blindly in the dark, looking for who the laughter was resounding from, but it was much too dark for him to tell if there was anyone there. All he could do was feel their presence. When he looked to the shadows, he felt there as someone or something there, something lurking purposefully in the dark- watching him, laughing at him. 'Two more to go choose wisely,' A blood-curdling voice whispered ever so close to his ear. The voice was the most terrifying thing Roland had heard and what made his heart skip a beat was that it wasn't a figment of his imagination. The voice came from right beside his bed. Roland woke up with fright. It sounded so real because it was. When he woke up, he saw something retreat from the side of his bed and into the bathroom. Roland curled himself up and shuddered at the sight. He was pale and drenched in sweat despite how cold the room was. Words could not describe the scurrility of the whole event and it was far from over with whatever had given him such a fright but hiding behind the door of his bathroom. Roland was trembling and could barely muster the strength to get out of bed, yet alone investigate. "Who's there…" He called, though his voice was no louder than a whisper.

He wanted to believe that it was all in his head but then he heard something fall over. Roland balled his fist as crippling anxiety gripped his heart. He had forgotten where the door was. He was too afraid to move. Even if he could, he was certain that whatever was in his bathroom would descend on him before he could make it into the hallway. A shape formed in the darkness; it was the kind of situation where despite everything being dark, he could still make out a menacing outline that was far darker than everything else. "Who are you?" Roland managed, "What are you doing in my room?"

Then he saw its eyes peer back at him. One was as red as blood, while the other was cold as ice, like a diamond, but he could tell they were eyes from how fixated they were on him. He tried to return the entity's gaze, but there was this knowing feeling inside him that if he did, he would be sucked into them, which would be the very end for him. Then it smiled. He could tell cause the pearly white rows of razors it called teeth seemed to glisten in the dark, although surrounded by such darkness, it looked smoky. Then he realizes that there was still power in his room. His lamp on the floor was still on and the light leaking in from under the door also illuminated a bit of the room but still, the bathroom should have been the brightest part of the room since he had intentionally left the light on with the door open out of habit, was the darkest. It was as though the light was being sucked out of the room and the longer the entity watched him, the darker the room got. Its darkness was coercive, like a growing shadow consuming all light in its part, until Roland was encased in a bleakness that he could no longer discern where he stood from where he should have. Roland couldn't tell what exactly it was he was staring at, but he knew for certain that it was the purest of evils. "What do you want from me?" He cried.

There was dead silence and then it laughed, the same horrible laugh from his nightmare. This time it boomed like it was coming from a megaphone like he was small and amusing to whatever was laughing at him. **"Everything…"** It's all too family voice responded.

IT WAS FAR FROM A GOOD MORNING. ROLAND'S HOTEL ROOM was trashed and reeked of booze and vomit while he laid sound asleep in bed, oblivious to the mess he'd made the previous night. Despite it all, the morning sun peering begrudgingly down on Roland's face through the hotel's large windows was really welcomed as Roland forced the sheets over his head. He was groggy, hungover, and so scared that even when he had fully awoken and was glad to find that it was just a nightmare he was having, he couldn't stop himself from trembling. It was lucid and yet it was the worst nightmare he'd ever had in all the years he'd spent alive. He wondered if the day he'd had was bad enough to so mess up his psyche that it caused him such a fright and then he rolled over to find blood on his sheets. Roland froze and paled at the sight of the blood on the sheets before he jumped out of bed so quickly that he stubbed his toe on the corner of the small drawer beside his bed then fell. It happened so quickly he brushed the pain off and was eager to keep his distance from the bed, almost like he was afraid that whatever had scared him half to death in his nightmare was still hiding under the sheets. The aching from his toe did not occur to him as he continued to pull the sheets off the bed. On the perfectly white sheets or as perfect as could be for this dingy hotel, were several stains, a few brown patches from his merriment and irresponsible drinking and a small trail of crimson red that caught his attention. 'That's my blood…' Roland thought wide-eyed in horror; it wasn't a lot, but it scared him still as he stood there gripped by terror and was panting when his stomach churned with his dull ears beginning to ring. Roland managed to make it to the toilet bowl before he began to throw his guts up. He spent at least 20 minutes throwing up before he began to feel better but then he was a sickly green and felt almost like he'd been pulled out of that one scene in the exorcist. He was still heaving with dry wrenches as nothing more came out of him. He felt like something that had been chewed up and spat on the side of the road but compared to the dreadful feeling his nightmare gave him. He was glad to still be alive. Roland was almost certain that he was a goner, and as he thought so, he felt his hands shake. Trembling greatly with fear, that was when he saw the blood trickling down his finger. "The fuck…" Roland gasped.

As he stared at his bloody hand in shock, he slowly began to piece together the events of the previous night. He remembered finding the ring and putting it on. The ring must have nicked him while he was making a fool of himself. He also remembered getting drunk and playing around with it. Now that he thought about the dumb wish he'd made, he felt stupid and was glad no one was there to see how low he had truly fallen. He could barely remember his exact wish, but he knew it wasn't a good one. In fact, he was sure it would land him in more trouble than he could handle if word of it got out. Roland admired the ring but then he found himself troubled by the gems on it. What troubled him particularly was that one of the red gems on the ring seemed to have lost its color. He wondered how such a thing was even possible. He even became afraid that he had broken it somehow. Roland felt it was better to leave the ring alone until he was sober rather than having anything bad happen to it but when he tried to take it off, the ring wouldn't let him. Roland paused and grumbled at the thought, 'How the hell to get it off his finger?' Roland wasn't a fan of jewelry. With how oddly the ring clung to him, he began to wonder if it was some sort of fade he wasn't aware of. Maybe the ring was one of those pieces that are easy to put on but had a trick to getting off. He held his hand over the sink and allowed warm running water to wash the blood away while he stroked the ring. It stung like hell and hurt twice as much when he tried to get the ring off his finger. As Roland struggled desperately, he could have sworn he heard someone laugh from inside his room. It was the same menacing slow laugh from his nightmare, it sounded distant, but it still scared him half to death as he spun around to meet no one there. Roland felt paranoid as his eyes darted across the room. He could still hear the laughter; it was muffled, almost like it was coming from the walls. Roland found himself staring at the walls, listening to them. The laughter wasn't a delusion, it was all very real and that horrified him. He hurried to the side of the bed where his stuff was all sprawled about and waiting for him. He had put all thoughts regarding the ring at the back of his mind once again and figured he could get it off some other time, preferably back under the safety of his roof where he didn't feel like some invisible monster was toying with him from within the walls. He stuffed his laptop back into his briefcase and then his car keys too, then shrugged on his clothes quicker than a thief and darted across the room to the door. He was in so much of a hurry that he didn't care for how badly he stunk or how unkempt he looked. The sooner he was out of the hotel, the better he felt he would be. Roland was convinced the hotel itself was more to blame for his paranoia than he was. Just as he was about to grab the doorknob and be on his way, he was startled yet again by a banging coming from the other side of the door.

Roland froze in his tracks. He wasn't expecting any room service and especially not guests. After all, no one knew he was lodging there, to begin with. He wished the sound was all in his head and that he was overreacting, but as he held the doorknob, he heard a loud thump on the door again. "Mr. Roland Butler?" A voice called uncertainly from behind the door and Roland sighed in relief. He let out a breath he never realized he was holding in and was relieved at the voice of whoever it was behind the door. So long as it wasn't that thing from his nightmares calling to him, he had no qualms with answering and so he did. Roland opened the door and was met by two tall men in uniform. Roland hesitated and his heart sank, he wondered what he had done to warrant a visit from the police, but then he recalled Nicolai's incessant calls and how he had punched the man in front of a crowd of workers. He opened his mouth to defend himself but then he gagged and threw up what was left inside his stomach. All that booze with no food was not good for him. The morning was barely upon Roland, and he had thrown up on a cop. 'I'm screwed,' Roland thought, deflated, and he looked just as dejected as the disgusted Police officers scowling back at him.

AN HOUR LATER AND AFTER A QUICK SHOWER ROLAND found himself waiting in a large room with nothing but the table he was sitting at and two chairs. He was grateful that rather than simply hauling his ass to the station, they let him wash up first. The room he found himself felt oddly depressing though. Other than the table and mirror, he'd noted that the only door granting entrance into the room was smaller than an ominously large mirror not too far from it that stretched across the wall of the room. This was his first time in a police station, but he had seen something similar in a movie. He assumed there must have been people watching him on the other side of the mirror. He wondered if there are recording it too. He felt very uneasy to the thought of being watched by people he couldn't see, especially after his nightmare from that morning, but somehow he held himself from causing a scene. After all, he wasn't in trouble, so there was no point causing any. Earlier after the puking on the officer incident, the officers explained to him that there was an incident and they politely asked him to follow them back to the station to answer a few questions. They also gave him something for his hangover, so he was feeling a lot better. Roland was very anxious and wondering if Nicolai had intentionally made the situation worse for him. Thinking about all the legal work and lawyers a case against him would entail troubled Roland but he took a deep breath to calm himself down and figured he was better off not thinking too much about any of that. If he wasn't under arrest and all they needed were answers, then he wished he could have refused them rather than sitting in a lonely room on the verge of a panic attack. The door finally came open and a tall dark man came in holding two cups. "Cappuccino?" He asked as he offered Roland one of the cups in his hand and though hesitant at first, Roland obliged.

"Thank you…" Roland replied as he gulped down without hesitation. A warm beverage was just what he needed to cool his nerves, and coffee was just what he needed to get his head straight

"That's a fine ring…" The man remarked and Roland felt he was put on edge. Every fiber of his body felt threatened by the statement, and he found himself glaring daggers at the man.

It felt almost as though Roland had been backed into a corner. The man noticed the animosity regarding the topic and figured he wouldn't press on about the ring. He assumed it must have been some sort of heirloom or, at the very least, something precious to Roland. If only the man knew just how much Roland hated the piece of Jewelry that had refused to release his finger. "Why am I here? Did something happen?"

The man was amused. He didn't dislike that Roland was straight to the point, in fact, he preferred it if things concluded smoothly and easily. There was bigger fish to fry and the sooner Roland was out of his doors, the sooner he could get back to work. Roland must comply as truthfully as possible for all that to happen. "I'm Detective Beckham from Central and I was brought here this morning concerning a peculiar case. I just need your help to tell if this is what I think it is,"

"And what do you think it is?" Roland gulped, 'Assault?' Roland didn't dare ask but in his heart, he had cursed Nicolai a thousand times over and the Detective noted that. He couldn't read Roland's mind, but he saw clear indications that Roland was nervous like he had something to hide, which gave him the impression that Roland was guilty of something. But then again, everyone has something to hide. Beckham kept that at the back of his mind moving forward.

"A murder."

Roland paled, looking a little sickly, although there was a little relief in his gaze, noted the detective.

"Who died?" He let out before another thought crossed his mind, "I want my lawyer-"

"Mr. Butler calms down," Detective Beckham said; the man's voice was husky and almost seductive. He seemed calculative, the kind of person that hardly ever made any mistakes and that scared Roland- because if there really was a murder, then it was a mistake bringing him in. Roland didn't murder anyone; he could barely even hurt a fly unless it was in his head of course. "Where were you between the hours of 10:30pm to 11:00pm."

"I was at a hotel. I had a rough day at work and so I refused to go home," Roland replied with certainty

"You own a Honda, right?" Detective Beckham smiled, "I prefer smaller cars. Yours was found parked a few blocks from your home, almost like you had deserted it."

"What's that supposed to mean? Why would I abandon it?" Roland scowled, "My car broke down, so I walked to the nearest hotel,"

"The Bay hotel is halfway across town. You're telling me you walked halfway across town to get a good nights' rest when you could have simply gone home?"

"I… That doesn't make any sense-" Roland hesitated with his mouth open as he tried to replay the previous night's events in his head, he was a bit tipsy after all his drinking, but he was certain that the hotel he slept in was a stone throw away from where his car broke down- or was it. He must have been really buzzed and way into his thoughts. His memories were far too fuzzy for him to say for certain.

'Why are they asking me all these questions? If there was a murder, why would I be a suspect? And even if I was… it wouldn't make sense to ask me why I deserted my car when I'm halfway across town, which means the murder occurred somewhere close to home' The query on his mind was visible on his face and just as he thought he began to piece the puzzle together. Then he was struck by concern at another thought, 'What if rather than close to home… the murder was at my home!'- "Helen, the kids… did anything happen to my wife? My family?!" he shouted worriedly.

Detective Beckham studied how distraught he became before he sighed deeply, and it was almost like his personality did a 180. He seemed apologetic, or rather he wanted to come off as apologetic, while he gave Roland the bad news but the calculating look in his eyes gave him away. "Your house was in flames last night Mr. Butler. There was no alarm, it must have failed, and firefighters would never have made it to the scene had your neighbors not noticed the blaze. It took all night to fight the fire but tragically, at the end of it all. The firefighters found four barely recognizable bodies underneath the rubble."

"Jesus…" Roland gasped as the names came to mind. He knew whose bodies the detective was referring to- 'Helen, Gerald, Mark and Marcus.' Roland was so dazed he sat back in his chair with his mouth open. He was on the verge of tears, not knowing how to handle such news that seemed to come all at once.

Roland felt like he was sinking deeper into his chair as the lights in the room grew brighter over his blank expression and the Detective noticed that. Roland was in shock. "Do you know anyone that would have done such a thing? Did you or Did Helen have anyone that would wish you all ill?"

"It was a fire… I wasn't home. Why do you ask?" Roland asked dazedly, he wanted to probe the detective for why he was a suspect but before he could ask and have Detective Beckham elaborate on his suspicions, their time together was brought to an abrupt end. The door swung to the room opened again and this time, three other officers came into the room. Roland didn't pay attention to their faces; he could barely raise his head higher than the tabletop. Besides, they were there for him. Instead, they wanted a word with the Detective. Beckham excused himself and went over to talk to them by the door. They were coming from the Bay hotel, where they'd picked Roland up and all confirmed that the hotel's surveillance cameras had footage absolving Roland of all suspicions. It proved Roland had checked in hours before the incident and that was a good enough Alibi to let him be on his way. There were no cameras in the room, that would have been a breach of privacy and yet the Detective seemed disappointed at the thought. With his innocence proven, Roland was free to go and was escorted out of the station. Roland was relieved that there was no case against him, but he found it difficult to relax in such a situation. He looked like a husk of a man, drooping like a depressed ghost all the exit. He was still in a daze and once he was outside alone, he started to think back to what could or who could have caused such a ghastly incident. His mind went to Marcus. If it were a murder, then it must have been his wife's lover- No… Marcus was dead too. That didn't make any sense. Roland didn't know what to think; the only logical conclusion he could reach was that the Detective was an overly cautious freak. 'Detectives are like that,' Roland thought to himself, 'Everything's a murder until proven otherwise.' Roland clawed through his head of hair frustrated by the sudden events of the day and suddenly he felt his finger get caught in it. 'Owww.' He groaned as he pulled his hand away and glanced to find the ring still clinging to the hair he'd just pulled off. Roland froze in his tracks staring intently at the ring in his hand. 'It couldn't have…' He mouthed as he recalled his wish in utter terror and disbelief. "It can't be true…" He muttered to himself as he crumbled on the side of the road, almost ignorant to the scorching sun above him, "No… no, no, no! no!!- this is impossible."

Wishes and magical rings don't exist. This thing on his hand couldn't have possibly killed his family or could it? Roland didn't know what to believe. All he had was paranoia and doubt as he quaked in his shoes.

"You look down in your pits Mr. Roland," An all too familiar voice called gently to him as the strange man from the bar held an umbrella over him to shield him from the sun.

Roland glanced at the man. He was filled with so many emotions, but fear was not one of them. The strange man before him raised a lot of questions in his head. There were answers he needed but seeing the convenience at which the only person with said answers had appeared to him, Roland was starting to 'believe'. "I never got your name?" Roland asked,

"Call me Bagmeth…" The man replied as he helped Roland back unto his feet. "Would you mind if we grab ourselves some more drinks?"

Roland was hesitant at first. He had questions and the confidence in the strange man's eyes implied that he had answers. So, Roland obliged.

# CHAPTER

## FIVE

Tragedy always has a way of bringing people together. Roland didn't have a lot of family nor friends; Helen was all he had. Now that he thought about it, he realized that with his family gone he was truly alone in the world. Roland hated to admit it, but deep down, he still loved his wife. He missed her, but he understood that there was no bringing her back. Helen was an only child, but she had a shit ton of relatives. Cousins, Siblings and Uncles who all didn't trust Roland one bit. Roland was like a ghost. He was so pale it was almost as though he didn't truly exist. He didn't social nor cry. All he did was linger over the caskets where whatever was left of his family laid. There was animosity about the way everyone looked at him. Roland could feel it. He couldn't blame them; he knew that their deaths were his fault. Most of them were simply sad and looking for someone to blame. 'If he were home, then maybe they would have all lived,' Someone muttered under their breath within earshot of Roland. He didn't know what stories they'd heard, and he didn't care either. None of it was true, but if they knew the truth, then they would not have hesitated to tear him limb from limb. Roland lingered over his wife's casket the longest at the funeral. He'd seen a picture of what was left of them. His boys were nothing more than char, but Helen's body was different. It looked as though she were wailing. Where eyes should have been had become nothing more than black holes and her mouth was open in a frozen scream. It must have been agonizing; Roland wondered if what was left of her would still look like it was in pain if he were to lift the casket open and get a glimpse at her. It had only been two weeks since the tragedy and though they had their ups and downs, he found that he missed her dearly. Roland took a deep breath and stroked the ring on his finger before letting it out. This was all very tragic to him, but he was willing to live with the choices he had made. He felt everyone hated how calm he was. Roland was a man who had just lost everything and yet he hadn't shed a single tear. Instead, he was strolling about the funeral like a changed man. 'Grief does that to a man,' Another voice had whispered but they were wrong. If there was anything within Roland's heart, it would have been guilt, not grief.

Despite it all, Roland felt grateful for the opportunities the ring presented to him. He had Bagmeth to thank for his newfound resolve. Now that he knew the rules and just how to get what he wanted, he had been lingering on the fine line between greed and morality. Roland used to be a skeptical man, but after what he had seen, there was doubt left in his being that there were greater powers at work. He wanted the truth and Bagmeth gave it to him. The ring on his finger was far from an accessory. It was a true treasure. Its power to bend reality to its bearer's liking was second to none. The Rose diamond was probably the most precious jewel in the world and now Roland had the hour of bearing it. He would not let his mind be clouded by trivial things such as guilt and fear. All he needed was to 'Believe and behold.'

After the police took him in, Bagmeth came to him. He followed the strange man to a pub on a whim. Roland wanted to know everything about the ring; in fact, he wanted to get the gem off his finger at the time, but that was before he learnt the truth. He had so many questions and Bagmeth was almost all-knowing, giving him the answers he sought almost before he had even bothered to ask. Then when he thought he'd learnt all the truths he needed, Bagmeth gave him more. From their conversation, he learnt just how powerful the Rose diamond truly was. Roland felt like a fool and was struck by guilt when he was forced to confront reality. The tragic deaths were his fault. There were the results of his wish. A part of Roland had already pieced that all together, but he wanted to believe that he was innocent, that none of that was his fault. Roland was distraught. To put it plainly, he was no different from a ceramic bowl that had been dashed against the wall. Roland could already feel the guilt eating away at him, but then he realized that there was no point to any of such emotions. Bagmeth showed him the way. Bagmeth consoled him for his error and with the wise man's guidance, he saw that there was no point to it all.

'A man will crush his fair share of ants…' Bagmeth said; everyone who died for Roland's sake should have been honored. He felt they should have been honored; this was the thought that kept him from falling apart. Even then, Roland still feared the ring's power. He felt overwhelmed and sought to return it. His life was in shambles, but he felt that with his wish granted, he could simply pick up what was left and make do from scratch. Bagmeth refused. It was when he tried to give a ring back that he finally learnt the rules of the Rose diamond. **Rule #1**: Once a bearer has been found, they cannot remove the ring until you have either made all three of their wishes or passed the ring on to a new bearer. Other than that, the bearer would have to die to revoke the ring. **Rule #2**: Wishes cannot be undone. **Rule #3**: The bearer cannot wish for more wishes. **Rule #4**: The ring cannot be destroyed or lost; it would always return. And the **5**th and final rule, the one that troubled Roland, is that the bearer has 30 days in between each wish to make another. Failure to comply would immediately forfeit their soul to Bagmeth.

The clock was ticking and Roland needed to make another wish. At first, Roland was worried that all the deaths would somehow trace back to him. Detective Beckham's intuition was frightening. The fact that he had brought him in to answer a few questions long before he'd even made sense of the whole ordeal gave Roland the impression that with enough time to build up a case, it was only a matter of time before the Detective would return for him. The Detective was very suspicious of him long after he left the station, but in the following week, Roland learnt that the wishes he made were absolute. He didn't have to worry about a fix; the ring had already prepared one in advance. His old boss, Nicolai, was found guilty of the murder of his family. Roland was in a daze at first when the news came to him. When he heard the details of the police's findings, he saw that just as he had wished for all of them to suffer, judging from how horridly Nicolai parted from this plain of existence, he feared that it had been just as horrible for his family's demise. Supposedly, Nicolai had gone to his house the night of the fire and when police began to search for him as a suspect, they tracked him down to a lake house on the outskirts of town and found that he had gouged out his eyes and swallowed them before disemboweling himself with a kitchen knife. The whole scene was so disturbing and grotesque that everyone involved in the investigation concluded the man was deranged with hatred for Roland. Something must have really sent him over the edge- he snapped and gone over to Roland's home hoping to harm Roland and in Roland's absence, he took out his frustrations on the family… and so Roland was now the victim of his tragic story. His wife's parents came to him in tears, trying their very best to console him and give him strength while they were the ones who were really falling apart. Losing their only daughter and grandkids at such age must have been crippling for them. As Roland watched them cry and crumble, he felt nothing. His biggest regret was that the ring had taken his boys from him. Other than that, he was disappointed he wasted a wish on all of them. "I need some air…" Roland declared when all the sadness he had caused grew too much for him to bear with a straight face.

He stepped out of the funeral home and retreated to the sanctuary of his car, where he found himself panting like he had just run a marathon. It felt like he was being chased when there was no one there to chase him. Roland had a myriad of thoughts in his head. After he had taken a breather, he glanced at the ring. People hardly noticed how he never took it off, not that he could. Getting it off his finger would have been no different was losing the finger. At first, he panicked and cursed the day he had crossed paths with the man, Bagmeth but now his impression had softened. With time he grew into an understanding with the man. There was only one logical explanation for it all, he was special. He had to be special for the ring to have chosen him. The ring chose him for a purpose. He was different from all the other ambitionless drones strolling about the streets like mindless zombies. It was just as Bagmeth had said, they were ants, and he was the one above them all what they saw as a loss was merely a step in the right direction for Roland. He smirked as he reached for his wallet and saw that he barely had enough money in it to afford a room at the run-down motel he had been staying for the past weeks. Sure, he had started his journey to greatness, but he still had not made his second wish yet. Roland didn't want to be too hasty with his wishes or he felt they might get out of hand. He was exasperated and hungry. It was then he knew what his next wish was going to be. Roland trailed his finger over the red gems of the ring. Now that he paid closer attention to them, he realized how ominous they really were. The skulls were so finely crafted that there was no doubt in his being that they were modelled after actual human skulls. For all he knew, they could have been from shrunken heads. Staring into the black gem had the exact opposite effect as the red gems. The red gems were alluring and seemed to beckon to everyone who laid eyes on them, but the black was different. They were scary and depressing; staring into them would fill you with dread. A horrible sense of foreboding warning you off the path of the rose diamond but by the time a bearer had laid their eyes on the black warning, it was much too late. Once you'd made your first wish, it was hard to turn your back on the promises ahead simply. He wondered if he would have accepted the ring if he knew how horribly things would turn out. 'This is for the best…' Roland thought to himself with a sigh. He feared that things would easily get out of hand if he wasn't being specific with his wishes. Sure, he had lost his family, but he had also gotten what he wished for. Nicolai was never going to ruin any of his days anymore. That at the very least, counted as a win. Roland felt that he could get the best out of his wishes with a calm mind. A good minute went by with him simply staring lastly at the ring, arranging his thoughts, and thinking through his options. "I wish for immense fortune and wealth," Roland whispered into his ring.

He felt that if he made his wish simple, there would be no ground for misinterpretation. However, when another gem on the ring lost its color, he gulped in fear at the thought of how wrong everything could go. It was like clarity that only came after making a horrible decision. Before he had the chance to regret his decision, he heard horrid laughter coming from inside his car, the same one that had plagued his dreams. Roland spun in fright with his fist balled in defense, more than ready to throw a punch at an intruder if he needed to but when he turned, there was no one there. The air was cold, and the vehicle was so silent that Roland could hear his heart pounding inside his chest, yet he found that he was all alone in the vehicle. Then a ringing startled him half to death. "Geez!" Roland cried out with his hand over his chest. He felt like his heart was about to burst out of him. The ringing was coming from the new phone he had got a few days ago, since the old one was damaged beyond repair from his outburst at the hotel. He managed to calm down and took the phone up to glance at its screen. It was an unknown number calling. "Hello…" Roland sighed into the phone.

"Mr. Roland Butler… My name is Eunice Biggins calling from the insurance company…" A soft voice greeted me from the other end of the line. Roland drifted off into thought as a wicked grin spread across his face. All he could do was stare at the ring on his hand while she spoke of the insurance payout for his family and home insurance. Soon after her call, he got a couple more calls regarding a settlement for the faulty alarm system within his home. Then there was his severance pay and several reimbursements that he had no clue about. Suddenly, people were calling him to hand him money. Just as he had wished for, Roland was rich in the blink of an eye.

TIME SEEMED TO FLY BY. ROLAND WAS LIVING THE HIGH LIFE but not even all the money in the world was enough to buy him the peace of mind that he sought. Sure, he had more money than he could hope to spend, but he'd been having a reoccurring nightmare ever since his second wish. One where a monster he never truly sees keeps counting down to something. Roland would wake up shaken and pale, it didn't make sense at first but slowly, he finally got a grasp of what was going on. From the comfort of his new private suite at the Valor Hotel, he sipped gin from fine glass and beamed at the ring on his finger. He owed all his glory to the damn ring, yet now that he had gotten his wish, he wanted nothing to do with it. The black gems on the ring seemed too ominous for him to ignore. Now that he looked at the ring more closely, he began to wonder what he had seen in it the first-day Bagmeth revealed it to him. The past two weeks were like a dream. After he got his insurance money, the rest was history. It felt like money just kept flooding into his account from heaven knows where. He could never trace the money back to a source, so he decided to put the money to good use rather than be warry and lose time cracking his head over a serious mystery. First bought a fancy hotel that happened to come with a casino, then a new car and after he was satisfied, he even sent Helen's parents a couple of million dollars out of guilt, but the money never ran out. Roland didn't look at price tags in the market anymore, all he did was want and the money got it for him. Instead of decreasing due to Roland's insane spending habits, the money he had access to only seemed to multiply. What marveled Roland the most about the whole ordeal was that he never got any calls from the bank or the police or anybody at all. No one seemed to care how he had gotten so rich so quickly and neither did they care to know where it kept coming from. Bagmeth's presence kept Roland feeling uncomfortable. He hadn't heard from Bagmeth and once in a while, he could actually catch some shut-eye without having any of the weird dreams that usually plagued him. The thing from his dream was more like a reminder, counting down the month till his next wish.

Roland was satisfied; he had more money than he needed. He felt like, in the weeks that had gone by he had probably become one of the richest men in the world and he wasn't going to let the ring take that from him. He didn't have the third wish and he had no interest in wasting it on something pointless. Roland had his suspicions that if he went for a third wish, the ring would take all it had given him in exchange for it. Every fiber in his body was itching to be rid of the dreadful ring, but the only way to do that was to find the ring a new bearer. With a confident grin, he wore a shirt and decided to head down to his casino, 'Finding a new bearer will be a piece of cake,' Roland thought to himself, and with all the influence he had, he meant it.

IT WAS JUST LIKE ANY OTHER NIGHT. THE AIR WAS RANCID with desperation and pride. Roland took a deep breath and smiled at the crowd as a lovely young lady came over to welcome him. The sight of drunk men going big and going home broke put a smile on his face. He never was much of a gambler but now that he owned a casino, Roland couldn't blame anyone for getting as addicted to gambling as they usually did. Roland was like a vulture, hovering over the tables, looking for the right sucker to descend on. Roland wasn't a workaholic, 'All work and no play makes Jake a dull boy,' He smirked at the thought as he helped himself to several glasses of champagne and even started to smoke. An hour passed, and soon he had forgotten his objective and was on the edge of a stupor as he threw wads of cash about like he was king of the hill. Roland felt bigger than life itself, and everything was moving in his favor. Everything. "Son of a bitch!" Some man snapped as he sent another guy railing with a punch. He pounced on the man he had punch and was pummeling him when Roland noticed all the commotion. He was strict about violence within his casino and was glad that before he needed to lift a finger, three hefty men in black jumped in and broke the fight up. "That rat's cheating!" The other man yelled and struggled with the men holding him as Roland approached them.

He wanted to give them a piece of his mind. Roland hated troublemakers unless, of course, he was the one causing trouble. Roland was close enough to smell the liquor in the furious man's breath. Then he heard an all too familiar voice. "I wasn't cheating, I swear! Not my fault your luck's for shit!" The other man retorted the other man that just happened to be Donald Sutton- his old colleague. Roland was some good feet away from them and usually wouldn't have batted an eye at the dilemma. He would have simply let his men work. Then a light bulb lit up in his head; why go through all the trouble of convincing a total stranger to take a mysterious ring from him when he could get onto the fingers of an old acquaintance far easier? With a wicked glint in his eyes, Roland decided to intervene in Donald's case. For his own selfish sake. "Calm down boys…" Roland chuckled to his guards. He stuffed several dollar notes in their pockets and grinned, "That's for doing such a good job, but I can handle it from here."

The men nodded and released the two gamblers before they excused themselves. "Mr. Butler…" The furious man gasped; he looked like a scared pup with its tail between its legs as he bowed, while Donald, on the other hand, was petrified at the revelation. Donald looked like he had seen a ghost and that delighted Roland. The universe had once again rolled its dice in his favor.

"It's fine… shit gets heated all the time," Roland excused the man, and he was genuinely relieved. He left in a hurry but not before he had shot Donald one last lingering glare. Donald didn't know what to say. He was embarrassed to be seen in such a place after how honest and moral he'd seemed back when they still worked together. "Mr.-" Donald bowed to apologize but Roland stopped him and threw a hand over his shoulder like they were a pair of old friends.

"Still as uptight as ever, I see," Roland laughed as he led Donald away from the bustling and hustle of the main casino grounds. "Come have a drink with me."

Roland insisted of the young man and of course, Donald couldn't do anything but comply sheepishly after the huge help Roland had just been to him.

# CHAPTER

## SIX

Roland's Casino was pretty large and descent. To the far end of the Casino was a small V.I.P lounge where Roland and his high rollers used to hang out. It had a mini bar with several large cushions and tables for games. That evening it was empty save for the sexy hostesses on duty that didn't hesitate to smother Donald and Roland in attention the moment they arrived. Being seductive was their occupation and fools making the error of falling for their charms was good for business. Donald looked like a mouse in a lion's den, he seemed to shrink with every step he took and that put a wicked grin on Roland's face. 'Welcome to paradise' Roland thought pompously, admiring all that he had accomplished in so little time. He had literally gone from grass to glory overnight but with one glance at the young man, he was left disappointed; he expected to see Donald cooing with awe at it all. Instead, he was shocked to find that Donald didn't seem to be enjoying himself and especially not the ladies' company. Roland scowled at first but then he brushed it off as a simple misunderstanding. The young man felt uneasy and out of place from the moment they arrived in the V.I.P lounge. Everything was so fancy and eye-catching it simply left him speechless and anxious. Roland's extravagant display of wealth only made Donald feel small. After all, he was leagues out of Donald's level and seeing how belittling his display of wealth affected the young man-made Roland smirk. Showing Donald how insignificant he was and making him feel insecure was just what he needed to do to make talking him into getting the ring off his finger easier. "Ladies… Give my good friend and me the room," Roland chuckled, and the girls chorused a sad pout before leaving with smirks. Donald and Roland were finally alone, and Roland decided there was no better time for the two of them to have a drink. He brought out a fancy bottle of wine he'd been saving at the mini bar and served two glasses.

"Fancy a drink?" Roland asked as he did, and Donald obliged him politely. He accepted the drink with both hands, Roland noted. It made it all the more obvious that he was nervous and that was just what Roland wanted.

"Thank you," Donald nodded. The wine was semi-sweet and dry, Donald wasn't a fan of wine, but he could appreciate a good drink when he had one. At first, they drank in silence. The music coming from the main casino was almost like a lull in the air and then Roland struck up one trivial conversation after another. Nothing too serious, the weather, his thoughts on the hotel and casino- modest things. When Donald had begun to liven up a little Roland then decided to probe him a little. He was honestly curious to know why Donald was in his establishment and more so to lay the ground for his true intentions. "What brings you to this side of town?" Roland asked,

Donald paused and seemed to shrink into his chair at the question. He gulped loudly as he put the glass of wine aside on a small stool and replied. "Well… things haven't been so great since you left the company." Donald continued, "When I heard what the boss had done to you… to your family. I was just so afraid- I had to leave."

"So, you quit?" Roland chipped in almost excitedly, 'What an idiot!' He laughed internally but in reality, he wore an Oscar-worthy façade of concern and empathy. He derived a cruel glee from knowing someone else was having it rough, especially because that someone else was the all too perfect Donald Sutton that he so envied. Donald nodded and then returned to his glass of wine, almost like it was the only thing that could quench a thirst he had. Roland did not hesitate to refill Donald's glass as the young man continued his narration. "Everything went downhill from there, I'm afraid. My girlfriend left me, I've been having trouble getting a new job and with my landlord breathing down my neck, I decided to come here. I was hoping to hit it big or something… I was naïve. I shouldn't have come here; who am I kidding-"

"Don't be so hard on yourself." Roland consoled him, "If you hadn't come here, we never would have met."

Donald nodded and then Roland began to stroke the ring on his finger. The ominous black gems didn't scare him anymore; Roland knew in his heart that he had already gotten rid of the accursed thing.

"Do you believe, Donald?" Roland queried,

"In God?" Donald asked with a puzzled look on his face. The question came at him from out of the blue and he honestly couldn't wrap his head around Roland's motive for asking such a question. "Yes, I do-"

"Then that makes what am about to do easier." Roland cheered as he held his ring finger out in front of the man and just as he was entranced by the gems the first time, he laid eyes on it; Donald was just as mystified. Seeing the way, the ring entranced people through another person's eyes was an eye-opener for Roland. How quickly the ring could get the best people to lust after it was almost scary. The experience was thrilling and Roland smirk in relish at it as he let Donald hold his hand. He felt like a king and Donald was but a jester in his eyes. The fool to keep him entertained. The room only added to the atmosphere. After all, gambling rings were designed to encourage bad decisions.

"That's a lovely ring." Donald cooed from his trance and Roland smirked.

"Take it…" Roland instructed as Donald did just that. The ring came off Roland's finger without the slightest resistance. It was just as easy as taking the ring from its case. Roland doubted that said ring had been the same one he had a pain dealing with just days ago. "Go on… wear it. It's yours now."

"Wait… Roland do you really mean that?" Donald asked. He was baffled by the gesture. He didn't feel like he deserved it. If only he knew what he was getting into.

"Someone gave it to me," Roland smirked, "I'm merely passing it on. Now wear the ring; you're its new bearer now."

As Donald wore it, he winced in pain at the ring pricking him. Donald was startled at first. He wondered if there was a sharp edge hadn't noticed or something and then he watched in awe as the color magically returned to the black gems right before his eyes. There were now three red gems adorning his index finger. "That ring might just be the best thing to ever happen to you, and so long as you follow the rules, you have nothing to fear."

"Rules…" Donald muttered, "What rules?"

Roland didn't answer; he was so relieved to be rid of the ring that he acted as though Donald was suddenly nonexistent. He strolled over to a counter and poured something stronger for himself. Roland wasn't a big fan of wine, but he was glad Donald was.

"You have three wishes, Donald," Roland smirked as he walked out of the V.I.P lounge with a pompous spring in his step and left Donald to his thoughts. "Make the most of it, and yeah… help yourself to all the drinks you like. You've earned it."

Words could not describe how confused Donald was as he watched Roland leave. He thought they were getting along famously, but now he didn't know how to feel about the entire encounter, especially about the ring that now clung to him.

IT WAS ONE OF THOSE DAYS WHERE THE DAY WAS SHORT, AND the night felt shorter. Roland was almost convinced that he was losing time. It was an odd thought, and it didn't last long on his mind. To him, the night was young and there was still plenty of time to get shit-faced and high. Roland felt that he deserved to celebrate a little after his successful endeavor. Rather than drink himself to stupor in the midst of his adoring fans, he decided to go for something a little tamer. He wanted to enjoy something that didn't involve alcohol, sex, or anything illegal. Roland felt he should enjoy the privileges of owning a hotel for a change. Funny how he owned such a large establishment and watched it thrive though he never moved a finger towards running it. Roland felt he had hired the most capable people to do all the heavy lifting for him; honestly, he had. He returned to his suite in high spirits and ordered a five-course meal that was set in his room while he took his glorious time soaking in his private hot tub. He didn't give a damn about what sort of mischief Bagmeth and his dreadful ring could cause. Thinking about how on edge he felt the day's prior because of being in possession of the ring put a grim look on his face. 'I'm glad that's over…' He thought contently with a long sigh of relief. He was more relieved to be rid of it. With the ring gone, he could finally focus on living his life to the fullest. In his words, he had eaten his cake and still got it. There was nothing in the world that could sour his mood, nothing other than the smirk on Bagmeth's face as he lingered over the hot tub like a lost housecat.

"Geez!!" Roland gasped with a spring in his step as Bagmeth laughed. "You scared me!"

"You seem to be having a good time," Bagmeth smirked. His eyes were unnerving; Roland couldn't look him in the face without recalling the horrible entity from his nightmares. Funny how the thing that intrigued him the most about the strange man was also the one thing he feared the most about him. Roland wanted to know how Bagmeth had gotten into his suite but then again, he realized how pointless asking would have been. 'He's Bagmeth after all,' that thought seemed to sum everything up nicely. Roland concluded and shrugged, "Shouldn't you be off haunting someone else?" Roland leered at Bagmeth, "If you hadn't noticed, I gave the fucking ring away-"

"Oh, I noticed…" Bagmeth grinned at him as he got out of the tub and scrambled for a towel. He felt exposed enough dressed in front of the strange man. Seeing him brazen was the last thing Roland wanted. "I also noticed that you forgot to tell him the rules."

"You didn't tell me the rules, not until after I had the fucking ring on. Does it matter? The ring is his problem now," Roland retorted; he truly believed that, but the smile Bagmeth wore at that statement of his was troubling. "So, what do you want from me now?"

"Nothing, really. To be honest with you Mr. Butler. I only stopped by to say goodbye." Bagmeth swore, "Who knows how long it'd be before our paths cross once again."

Bagmeth looked concerned but Roland could see beyond his devilish theatrics. "We are never going to meet again. I'm done with my wishes and I'm grateful, so leave me the hell alone."

"You only made two wishes Roland, and Money can't buy you everything," Bagmeth smirked as Roland turned to return to his room, he was done with the conversation and was more than eager to see Bagmeth off his property as soon as possible but the moment he turned his back on Bagmeth an illogical fear gripped his heart. The fear was so intense that it immobilized him. He felt like he was standing in the presence of a feral creature on the verge of pouncing. His muscles stiffened and he could have sworn something was breathing down his neck. Roland broke into a cold sweat and squeezed his eyes shut. He didn't want to die and neither did he want to know what was behind him. That was when a voice came to him. It was Bagmeth's voice and yet it wasn't; the voice was much more menacing when it said, 'You look pale…'

Roland fell to his knees as a cold breeze blew over him and when he turned, Bagmeth was gone. He was all alone, and Roland sighed in relief. Roland was finally free of the ring and Bagmeth. Now he could live a full life and forget all about his horrible encounter.

ONE THING LED TO ANOTHER AND BEFORE ROLAND EVEN realized it, a week had gone by, the best week of Roland's life. The week that followed was nothing short of bliss for Roland. His days were riddled with fun activities and functions. His nights were now meant for parties and clubbing. Eventually, Roland realized he'd hardly slept in days. He couldn't sleep with all the excitement he was having; when he fell asleep or passed out drunk, he would have nightmares. Persistent reoccurring nightmares of the most grotesque things. He thought with the ring gone, the nightmares would follow, but with time they only grew more distasteful and haunting. Roland didn't know who to blame or what to do about it either, so he hardly slept. Roland bounced from coffee to one drug or the other to starve himself of sleep and then he distracted himself with all the company and goods money could buy. Soon he deluded himself that he didn't sleep because he didn't want to. He didn't see the need to. Telling himself, all this made it easier for him to pass the time a lot more than accepting that something wasn't allowing him to rest stressed him. Roland became a literal party animal. He partied day in and day out, and when there weren't any parties and he felt lonely, he would sate his lust with all the beautiful women that were half his age who all flocked to his side by the dozens. If he wasn't drunk, then he was high on one drug or the other. Roland had become the textbook definition of a playboy and soon became the talk of the town. Everyone knew what he was up to at any given the time of day and yet no one knew who he was. No one ever cared to ask how he'd gotten so rich. He could have been the richest man in the world and still hadn't made it onto a billboard. Roland was the popular nobody that everybody knew. With time he had even forgotten about Helen and his kids. What were their names? - So long as he could remain as happy as he had already become, nothing else mattered.

At the peak of all his glamor, he suddenly developed an odd quirk. He couldn't go a day without stuffing several painkillers down his throat every morning. He didn't do it for a rush or some high; he did it because it was the only way he could cope with the pain he was suffering. He was extremely fatigued and paled from lack of sleep and now depended on painkillers for the frequent headaches he'd constantly been having for a while. Before Roland noticed, he found himself being nauseated out of the blue at odd hours of the day. There was no pattern to his symptoms, nothing that could be diagnosed as part of something bigger immediately. So, when he first saw the symptoms, Roland wanted to believe that maybe he had partied a little too hard. Roland found it funny that all his wealth had clouded his thoughts to the point that he almost forgot he was still very human. He continued to party. He tried to shake up his schedule. It gave him the illusion that he was building a healthier lifestyle and when he felt a little ill, he decided to lay off the alcohol for a bit before going hard at it at the drop of a hat. When he finally did put a stop to all of his excessive partying, he then decided it was time to take his glory to a whole new level. Roland decided to expand his financial empire by going into Real estate.

He had no trouble finding decent properties and setting up a business plan. Long before he had gotten his wish granted, he tried his very best to be attentive to the housing market's forecasts. With his growing fame, once he showed an interest in real estate, it was only a matter of time before several other investors had gained an interest in having talks with him. Roland scheduled a meeting with a few of them and was more than certain that it was going to be a big success. He was living on cloud nine and nothing was going to bring him down. The day of the meeting came quickly. Finally, the day was upon him, and he took Mark, Lauren, Nora- the three investors he hoped to impress, out on a cruise. He pulled all the stops with entertainers and food. He hoped to butter them up well enough that they'd feel foolish to turn him down. At the height of his Grande display, he led the entire meeting; he had gotten a lot more charismatic over the months. Rather, his money made him look so, but tragedy struck just as they were about to come down to a proper agreement. Roland collapsed and passed out cold.

# CHAPTER
## SEVEN

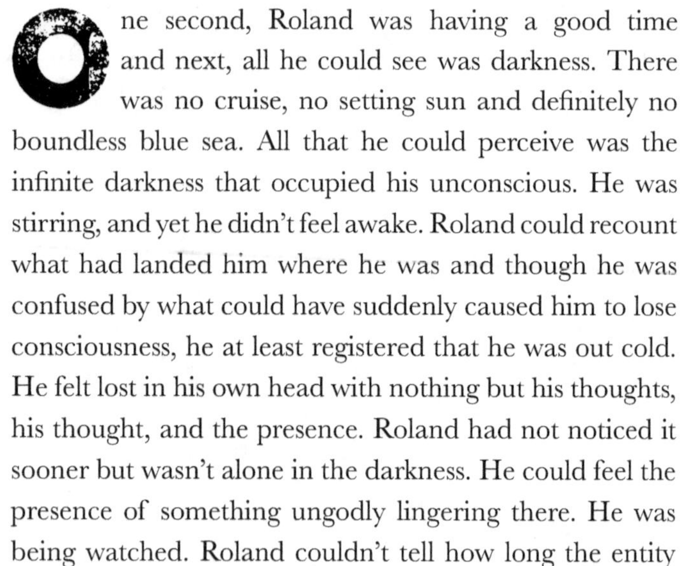

One second, Roland was having a good time and next, all he could see was darkness. There was no cruise, no setting sun and definitely no boundless blue sea. All that he could perceive was the infinite darkness that occupied his unconscious. He was stirring, and yet he didn't feel awake. Roland could recount what had landed him where he was and though he was confused by what could have suddenly caused him to lose consciousness, he at least registered that he was out cold. He felt lost in his own head with nothing but his thoughts, his thought, and the presence. Roland had not noticed it sooner but wasn't alone in the darkness. He could feel the presence of something ungodly lingering there. He was being watched. Roland couldn't tell how long the entity had gotten its eyes on him but when he heard it laugh, he knew that it was far from done with him. Roland woke up to find himself hospitalized with a horrible rash spreading across his skin. Apparently, he had been unconscious for days and was diagnosed with Leukemia, a blood cancer. None of it made any sense; Roland could have sworn he was healthy the last time he had visited the hospital. It didn't matter how long his last visit had been; Roland refused to accept the doctor's diagnostics. Alas, denial only caused him pain. His symptoms worsened and he found his face riddled with red pores and awful rashes; he felt disgusted to look himself in the mirror.

Roland was desperate, but he had not lost hope just yet. The investors he planned to meet with had fled the deal; they felt it was unwise to go into business with an ill-struck man. Roland didn't care for them in the slightest when he thought of it- he never needed their money. He still had a bastard fortune at his beck and call, one that he did not hesitate to squander. At first, he spent thousands on traditional treatments, consulting renowned specialists and travelling to the best medical facilities money could afford, but when that didn't seem to bear fruit, he went the extra mile and paid millions to afford the most promising experimental treatments. That only made things worse. His cancer was evolving. Before he realized it, he had skin falling off his face and pores oozing out a black slime. It wasn't blood nor pus; none of the doctors could explain it. They all insisted it was cancer but in truth, they had never seen anything like it. Soon, Roland's organs began to fail and all the medications in the world couldn't stop the agonizing pain he derived from merely breathing.

He had become a husk of a man. Roland was covered in so many bandages that he looked like a mummy.

Everyone became afraid of his horrid appearance, not to mention his stench. Roland smelt like a rotting corpse; before he realized it, no one wanted anything to do with him. Roland fell into a deep depression. Money wasn't a problem. Even at the doors of death itself, the money kept finding its way to him. 'Money can't buy you everything…' those words rang through to Roland. Bagmeth had done this to him. Roland cursed under his breath but felt that the ring would be his saving grace at his lowest. Roland set out to find Donald at once.

ROLAND DIDN'T KNOW WHAT CAME OVER HIM. HE GREW TOO tired of waiting for news on Donald's whereabouts and the liquor that usually comforted him only made him feel twice as horrible. He needed some air and so he got in one of his cars and told his driver to hit the highway with nowhere specifically on his mind. They went round town on a wanderlust-inspired drive and when his driver took a certain familiar street, Roland found himself glued to the window. "Take the next right…" He spoke.

"Excuse me sir?" His driver responded he wanted to be certain Roland had actually spoken. His tone made it far too easy to tell he was on edge. Being told to drive aimlessly was actually harder than many would think. Not knowing if the next intersection or how fast or slow you went was going to cost you your job or not. It was like being a computer with no instructions to render it pointless.

"Take a right and head straight," Roland repeated and the driver hid his smile as he followed Roland's instructions. He was new and all but that didn't matter to Roland. In fact, Roland was oblivious to how nervous his silence had gotten the young man. The man turned and went straight ahead until a mailbox came into view and asked the driver to stop in the driveway. Once they had parked, Roland didn't utter a word. He simply stared out his window with solemn eyes. The man cleared his throat, "Are you okay, sir?" He dared to ask.

Roland shrugged. "I'm fine… take me home."

"Will do, sir." The man nodded as they drove on. He was confused. Roland was sure that the young man was wondering why they had driven through such a mundane neighborhood for no reason; he had no clue that Roland used to live there. They stopped in a clearing where a house used to be; up until a month ago, that spot used to be a home with a garage where Roland would drive himself and be welcomed from work by his boys. He recalled how good his wife's cooking was, so good in fact he felt all the meals he had been getting at the hotel were over-glorified. Sure, they tasted great and all but none of them were like Helen's. Helen, his wife. Gerald and Mark, his sons. It felt like a dream. Thinking of how happy they all were together made him wonder how he had ever forgotten such a thing. All the guilt he had bottled deep inside came rushing out of him in tears as he palmed his face. He was tired and weak and alone. He needed the ring… with the ring, he could make himself feel whole again. Seeing what was left of what used to be his home was like a wake-up call to Roland; the problem was- He woke up to yet another dream, still dancing within Bagmeth's palm.

DONALD SEEMED TO HAVE FALLEN OFF THE FACE OF THE earth after their last encounter. No one seemed to know where he was or what he was up to. He was not an easy man for Roland to find. Locating him was so challenging that Roland began to wonder if he was mistaken. Maybe Donald didn't want to be found. The thought frightened Roland; he knew that if Donald had wished not to be found, then there was nothing he could hope to accomplish in searching for him. Roland didn't want to think about it. He was already pessimistic about his search but with his life on the line, he was determined to succeed regardless of the cost or how slim his chances appeared to be. It took Roland months, 12 private investigators and half his fortune to trace the man down. One of his investigators had tracked Donald to a small suburban home in a town Roland didn't bother recalling. He didn't care where he found Donald, all that mattered was knowing how to meet him. Apparently, Donald had gotten married over the period and lived a pretty modest life. Roland thought of Donald with nothing but disgust. He felt irritated that the man could have had anything in the world and yet he settled for something so simple. Roland did not waste a second. The moment he learnt where Donald lived, he set out immediately. He had one foot in his grave and was determined to have the ring before his time would run out. Donald and his wife both ran extra shifts to pay their bills. Most of the time, Donald would arrive home from work hours before his wife would. Not that any of that mattered to Roland, all that mattered was that he met Donald at this home. Roland could barely even walk straight at the time. He wore a large cloak over his bandages but even then, the black ooze stained his clothes and left a trail after him. Donald was in the living room of his house when Roland staggered up to the front door and slammed his fist on the door as hard as he could muster the strength to.

"My god…" Donald gasped in the doorway; he was startled by Roland's appearance. He had no idea who he was even looking at until he suddenly grabbed him by the wrist. "I think you have the wrong house, sir!"

"Donald, you sly bastard," Roland croaked, his voice hushed and almost inaudible. He sounded like a broken record player and every word out of his mouth hurt just as much as walking. "You don't recognize an old friend?"

Donald's lit up in horror when it dawned on him just who was at his doorstep. Roland tried to force his way in but then he tripped and fell forward towards the steps. Time seemed to swoon by slowly, had his head met the concrete, his frail skull would surely have parted and spilled his brains across the floor. Roland shut eyes; he didn't have the strength to stop himself. Roland had resigned himself to fate but then he noticed that a minute had gone by, and he was still alive and without a splitting pain in his head.

"What happened to you Roland!" Donald shrieked, to Roland's surprise. The young man had saved him, Donald was quick enough to catch him right before his head touched the floor. Roland was relieved but he was still in so much pain that he couldn't help but groan loudly from being held awkwardly. "Let me get you seated," Donald apologized as he carried Roland into the living room and sat him down. He hurried into the kitchen and returned with a glass of water.

"Thank you…" Roland greeted hoarsely as he glanced about the small home he had just been welcomed into. The place was sparsely furnished save for the hundreds of family portraits that adorned the walls about the flat screen over the fireplace.

"My place isn't much, but you can make yourself feel at home," Donald said sheepishly as he took the glass from Roland and placed it on the small table beside the couch he was in. Roland lazily browsed through the room; he hadn't realized just how thirsty he was until he had actually had something to drink.

"Do you have any fruit?" Roland managed. It felt humiliating that he had asked when he could have easily bought a million if he had just had the strength to reach for his checkbook. He saw Donald as odd with how delighted he seemed by the visit; it reassured him that getting the ring back would be an easy endeavor.

"Are you fine with apples?" Donald asked as he got out of his own seat and Roland nodded. Again, Donald disappeared from the living room and returned a moment later with a bowl full of clean water, a couple of apples and a small knife. Ronald forgot his manners as he immediately began to chew through one of the apples like a ravenous beast, but Donald didn't seem to mind. Instead, he had a very troubled look on his face as he watched Roland eat. Roland choked at one point and nearly knocked the bowl and knife over, but Donald rushed over and took them all away. Not an ounce of shame was left in Roland's heart as he glanced over to the fireplace and spotted what looked like a school trophy. He could tell Donald was curious about his visit but was being reserved about probing him and he, in turn, felt it would have been too rude of him to simply demand the ring after the small kindness he had been shown.

"Thank you…" He managed after clearing his throat disgustingly. His voice seemed to be deteriorating to a point it wouldn't be wrong to assume his lungs were in shreds. It was a miracle Roland was even still alive and able to walk on his own two feet. "Is that your sons…"

Roland pointed to the trophy and Donald chuckled a little as he itched at the back of his neck shyly. "No… they're actually mine."

Donald had his boyish laugh as he walked over to the trophy and brought it to Roland. "This was my parent's old place." Donald explained, "After I met you at the Casino, I became a changed man. I went after Monique, my parents gave me their old home and once we married, we both got new jobs and moved in here,"

"How wonderful…" Roland smiled genuinely behind all the darkened bandages that hid what was left of his face and thumbed the trophy's label as he did. "You sound satisfied…"

"I am, honestly," Donald assured him as he walked over to the bowl and cut an apple for Roland. He felt Roland wouldn't choke if the apples were cut thinner and Roland appreciated that, nodding as he accepted the apple from Donald. "What happened to you, Roland?"

Roland froze up as he felt his teeth pop out of his gum when he bit into the apple. Donald gasped and rushed to get a napkin. Roland could hear his ears ringing as Donald tried to clean the blood oozing from the side of his lip like drool. He was running out of time; he could feel it, which greatly scared Roland. He grabbed Donald by the hand and stared him in the eye. "You're so content with your wishes. Then you wouldn't mind returning the ring to an old friend. I'm running out of time... I need my last wish-"

Donald stared at him in shock and backed away. Roland tried to reach out again and nearly fell off the chair; the moment he leaned over, a black fluid trickled down his nose and unto the carpet. "Donald give me a ring; we don't have time for this."

"I never used that demonic thing!" Donald snapped. He looked pale and scared all of a sudden.

"What?" Roland paused. One could see the confusion on his face from the way he gaped at the young man in front of him in disbelief. It had not once crossed his mind that maybe Donald had not used any of his wishes. From the looks of things, it seemed very believable but even then, Roland was still stubborn. "What are you saying? Why not?"

"Why would I?" Donald rebuked, "I knew it was trouble from the moment it latched onto me-"

"So long as you follow the rules, you'd be fine! Bagmeth should have explained the rules-"

"I'm grateful that you gave me a ring thinking it would help but I didn't need it. That '**Thing**!' you call Bagmeth came after me, but I refused to let its words in my head. It couldn't deceive me." Donald hissed, "What have they done to you? Have you seen yourself in a mirror, Roland? Can't you see what it's doing to you? That thing is eating you and it's been trying to eat me ever since I wore the ring. Only Lord knows how many poor souls have fallen victim to this ploy, but never again. I've seen how dreadful this ring can be and I won't let it hurt anyone else. I swear it."

"That's great for you and all but if you don't want it, I do. Then just give a ring back!" Roland raised his voice and tried to get out of the chair, but he got up too quickly and that made him swoon, his ears rang louder, and he coughed up blackened blood as he knocked the plates off the table to his side. Donald rushed to his seat and steadied him. They didn't see eye to eye on the topic of the ring but that didn't make Donald any less concerned about his well-being. Donald was truly a saint and wanted to believe he had Roland's best interest in mind but none of that mattered. Not to Roland. He was on borrowed time; he was too afraid to let Donald's kind and reassuring words get to him so easily.

"I'll get you help; I won't let the ring or that thing take you. You've got to trust me on this Roland." Donald swore as he held the napkin, he brought out from his pocket to Roland's bloody mouth. "We'll find a way out of this. I only have the ring; I haven't made any wishes. The ring can't harm me, and I swear to God that so long as I live, it won't harm you either."

Roland was as stubborn as a goat but even then, he found himself being sucked into Donald's big bright eyes. There was nothing like Bagmeth's; there was nothing mystifying or bewitching behind them. Donald's eyes were as human as his, yet they mirrored the purity of his soul. The sincerity behind them was so pure it almost inspired him to be a better man. Roland wondered how dark his eyes had gotten; maybe if anyone were to stare into his eyes, it would feel no different from staring into the black of the rose diamond's gems. Donald held his hand to comfort him and then Roland saw it. What he had sought for so long was right before him. He saw that Donald was wearing the ring that very moment- Of course, he was; it wasn't like he could take it off. Donald was telling the truth; just as he had claimed, all three gems testified to the young man's innocence, with their bright red color looking as radiant and as bewitching as the day he had handed the ring to him. Donald wasn't spewing empty promises cither, he had a plan to put a stop to it all. All he needed was for Roland to actually listen to him. Donald was so confident that Roland actually felt safe in the young man's care. The man that Roland once despised was now a knight in shining armor to him. He wanted to believe wholeheartedly that there was still a chance for him. He'd given up so much already; the thought of salvation felt wasted on him. Would Donald really want to save him if he knew what Roland's wishes cost? If he knew about Helen and the boys… Roland wished he had never laid eyes on the ring in his heart. Maybe he would have been happier that way.

"It's going to be fine," Donald promised. Those words were just what Roland needed to hear to calm his raging heart. Donald made him feel at peace for the first time in months. Sorely, the peace he felt was short-lived. Roland found himself covered in goosebumps like a cool breeze had blown over his naked body. He was tense as there was this growing pressure at the back of his mind. Roland's eyes darted across the room; he could feel that they weren't alone. He was convinced that the shadows in the corner of the room had slowly begun to grow, and he could see it all happen when he tried to convince himself that it was all in his head, that he was paranoid and shouldn't have been. Roland wanted to convince himself that he was safe with Donald by his side, but his heart was long broken for faith to find home in it. All the courage he thought Donald had given him was nothing when he heard the horrible laughter that had always haunted him, but this time it was closer than always. It was coming from the walls around him, just like it did that day at the hotel when he first heard it. Roland was so afraid he would wet himself there and then. The wicked entity from his nightmares was more than a figment from his imagination and it was coming for him.

'…Don't be afraid. I'm with you… he can't hurt you. Trust me.' Donald's voice called to him. He could see Donald before him and yet Donald's voice came to him as though it were echoing from miles away. Roland had lost his sense of self. If he could flee in spirit and abandon his broken body where it sat, surely he would have. Roland didn't know where or when he was all of a sudden. All he knew was the desperation and fear slowly eating at him as a voice he prayed never to hear again spoke to him. **'Time's up…'**

Roland wailed. He could feel something in its chest, tightly ever so gently about his heart as though threatening to burst it. The entity he so feared was inside him. There was no escaping it, no escape unless-

"Arrgh! Wait! Please listen, Wait! I have one more w-wish… Donald, give me a ring!" Roland wailed in pain as his eyes shot frantically about the room and he held his aching chest. The fact that he wasn't dead meant that he still had a chance, and with every passing second, Roland grew more desperate and driven to escape death. Donald's voice couldn't reach him anymore; he was in a world of his own. A world governed by nightmares and pain. All Roland did hear was the laughing. It was loud and demeaning, like he was some sick joke to whoever was watching him.  All he felt was the knowing feeling of imminent demise and the tight grip in his chest threatening to crush his frail heart. He was trembling and muttering to himself. His body was hot enough to boil water; Roland had become a man possessed in every sense of the word. He couldn't see Donald anymore; all he could see was the darkness. Donald was desperate to help him, but he was just as confused and bewildered by the whole ordeal as Roland was. Neither of them knew what to do and neither of them could truly see each other. Roland knew Donald was still by his side. The pain had clouded his judgement, but he was certain. He kept crying and begging for the ring; his words came out in raspy, suffered slurs and Donald couldn't make any sense of it, but that frustrated Roland greatly. When Donald didn't seem intent on giving him a ring, Roland recalled he could get the ring if its current bearer was deceased and so he gave into his hysteria and lashed out viciously at the young man. Roland pounced on Donald and struck him. Roland didn't know where the strength came from. A moment ago, he could barely even stand upright and now he felt like he had the strength of ten men and the motivation to use it. The laughter and the grip on his chest wouldn't go away. Instead, it was almost ecstatic. Like whoever was watching was having a good show off of Roland's lowest. With each blow Roland landed on poor Donald's face, the laughter grew louder and he could feel the cruel entity's presence grow closer, more pronounced. It could have been a fearful thought at an object within the corner of his vision at first but slowly, it began to feel as though the entity was breathing down his neck. The vile thing was enjoying the spectacular as Roland threw his hand forward with so much force that he felt the bones in his finger break, yet dulled by fear, he roared on like a feral animal. Pounding away at what used to be Donald's face.

Fear was not all Roland felt. There was disgust and shame that welled up inside him. Regret berated his thoughts and slowly, guilt reined his sanity back in. Donald had nothing to gain from him, yet the young man was eager to help him out of the hole he'd dug with his own hands. None of his actions felt right and with that thought in mind, Roland slowly gained a bit of his sanity. He stopped himself in the middle of a punch, but it was much too late. By the time he had brought himself back to his senses, he found the bashed in face of Donald's corpse with the trophy he was holding unto a moment ago sticking out of where an eye should have been and the ring barely clinging to the poor man's finger. He was trembling when he glanced and saw the knife in Donald's hand. Yes, he had struck Donald first but with a blade, he was more than certain that Donald would have had no trouble killing a frail man. And yet Donald refused to do so. His kindness wouldn't let him - his kindness was his bane. Even with Donald dead, there was no time for relief. The fear that had pushed Roland to the very brink of insanity was still very present in the room. It was far from done with him. The room seemed darker. The lights that were still on flickered and the grip on Roland's chest grew unbearably tight. The evil presence still haunted him more so than ever now that Donald was dead- it was stronger even. Roland could feel it breathing down his neck when he stole the ring from Donald's hand and forced it unto one of his broken fingers without regard for the pain. '**Make a wish...**' The same voice that kept returning to him said. It wasn't a lull or a suggestion; it was an order from servant to master and in his fear, Roland had no time to thing or deny the voice what it demanded of him. He blurted out the first wish that came to mind without a moment's hesitation, anything to be free of the fear and agony he felt.

"I wish to not die!" Roland cried as he crumbled over Donald's body as if he was convinced that the young man could somehow protect him even in death. The walls began to tremble as though the wind was going wild about the house knocking things off their shelves and breaking windows. Then suddenly, there was silence. Roland was too afraid to get back up. He clung to Donald's body until he felt the last of his warmth leave him. He couldn't tell how many minutes went by, and then after a little more time, he finally gathered the courage to raise his head again. He finally saw the aftermath of his carnage with renewed eyes and could barely tell what he'd done from what the cruel entity that was with them had done. The pain in his chest was gone and yet he still felt very much in pain. Roland felt like a hollow man. He didn't cry. He had wasted too much time already. 'Ants…' He thought with one final glance at Donald's corpse. It was a terrible thing he'd done but it was a step towards his greatness- that made it a necessary sacrifice. He wanted to believe that Donald would forgive him. That must have been why he didn't kill him when he had the chance. Roland glanced at his finger and watched the color flush out of all three red gems leaving the most dreadful triad of gems he'd ever laid eyes on. It felt almost as though he could hear voices and cries softly leaking from inside the ring. Roland did not allow the ring's horror to frighten him, not there, at least. He knew he had to leave; it was only a matter of time before Donald's wife would return. The thought of how devastated she'd be returning to her home in shambles to find what was left of her husband just lying in a pool of gore and blood cause him to grimace. He felt no different from the monsters he fled from and even still, he took a deep breath and he left in a hurry. 'It had to be done,' He thought to himself, Roland had gotten better at lying to himself. The driver then had been waiting for him; it was the same young man that had driven him around town the last time he had fallen into depression and decided to visit what was left of his old home. The man looked troubled at first, but he kept a strong front for Roland. He didn't give a rat's ass about the stench or the blood on his employer. To be honest, he was too afraid of how easily Roland could make him disappear with a single phone call. In fact, Roland didn't need to kill Donald himself, but he feared that had anyone else come in contact with the ring, he would have lost all hope of getting it for himself. Roland had grown used to most people simply accepting his reality so long as it gave them a chance to line their pockets. The deed was done; Roland had gotten his wish. All he had to do now was wait and live a long, happy life.

# CHAPTER
## EIGHT

The room was filled with so much silence that many would doubt there was a soul within it. It was so silent that if anyone sat perfectly still enough, they could probably hear their own heartbeat, but Roland wasn't anyone. Even if he did so, he wouldn't hear anything. Roland had crawled into a corner and hadn't blinked in hours; he was like a mannequin with a deadpan outlook on everything around him. He was too afraid to do anything else. Roland felt relieved at first, getting home with all three of his wishes granted and no longer clinging to the fear of death. He thought it was all over and that the worst was finally behind him, but he was horribly mistaken. He believed the scariest thing he could find in his dreams were the eyes and the laughter from the one entity that always haunted him; he was wrong. It was the day after his trip to Donald's; he fell asleep and woke up someplace dark. It was almost like all his other dreams. First, there was silence. Then there would be laughter and then he'd find himself running for dear life until he managed to wake back up. This dream had nothing like that. Yes, there was the usual darkness but slowly, light began to creep in and then he found himself in a mundane living room with a small fireplace. Roland was confused. He couldn't shake the familiarity that the whole place had. It was more like a memory than a dream. In fact, despite how eerie it was, he thought he'd prefer it to all his other nightmares but that was only before Donald appeared. He was still missing a face and was holding a knife. Roland felt crippling guilt that literally petrified him. He waited for the inevitable, expecting Donald to kill him but Donald didn't. His deformed corpse simply stood there and watched Roland crumble as he desperately tried to escape. Then there was a fire. It grew from all around them, consuming the building and them both.

Even with his wish granted, Roland was far from happy. He had no peace and thinking about what his encounter with Donald's apparition meant was eating at his mind. After that night, Roland hardly did anything other than cower in the darkness of his room. Days turned into weeks and Roland was oblivious to just how long he'd spent holed up in his room; the meals he'd ordered had begun to rot and fester with maggots while all he did was sit there and watch. The reality was too cruel for him to face. He'd killed a man; the authorities were bound to be on his heel. He feared that when he decided to go outside, the police would take away to rot somewhere in a cell. He was afraid of confinement, so much so that he couldn't notice that he was already confined within a cell of his own making. Sure, he wasn't dead, that was what he wished for, but he wasn't feeling any better either. At first, he thought waiting would show results; ever since his nightmare about Donald, he'd only begun to deteriorate even more. Rather than heal, his body went numb. He was still very much in pain, but he could hardly feel it anymore. The disgusting black fluid that had oozed out of his body constantly had stopped oozing from his skin if what was left on his body could even count as skin. He was repulsed when he took his bandages off to look in the mirror. Roland hardly had a face left; water felt like flames when it came in contact with him. Roland hadn't washed himself in days and when the fluid began to ooze from his gums, he gave up on hygiene entirely. There was no perfume strong enough to mask his stench. He reeked of death. His fingers were in shambles, frozen in the awkward positions they'd taken since the day they had been broken at Donald's home. Roland could still remember the sensation of a skull caving in under his fists; he dared to watch the news and found that Donald's murder hadn't made it to any headlines. There were no police officers after him. It was almost as though it never happened. There were no consequences- 'Bullshit! This isn't real!' Roland clawed at his head, pulling off clumps of hair, many would have thought that he'd be gladdened by the revelation, but they would all be wrong. Roland didn't know what he wanted, but he felt as though he had already seized to exist. Even without the fear of the law descending on him, he feared impending doom. The impending doom that he was certain would seize him at

Bagmeth's next visit. Roland was so afraid that the way he carried himself from then on could barely count as living.

Roland hardly ate, He managed to keep his guilt at bay with the deception that his actions were logical but even that wasn't enough to help him sleep at night. He never went out or bathed; he was so confined to his room that no one even cared to bother checking on him. His room had become a world of its own; his staff never once rang him for anything, nor did room service ever bother to ask if he needed anything. It was like his room was never a part of the hotel, which added to his depression. Roland thought he didn't need anybody. He thought he'd always be content so long as he got what he wanted. He believed it would never matter how many people bit the dust for his sake. Now he was all alone, and the solitude felt as great a hell as the constant pain he was always in. Eventually, Roland managed to schedule an appointment at the last hospital he had visited. He'd kept to himself so long that he almost forgot how rich he was. He wasn't sure how much he'd spent to find Donald but on his return, he found his wealth had tripled since then. It was sad, he had all that money and now he saw no need for any of it. The wealth was wasted on him, and he knew it. His appointment was set for a weekend, but patience was far from one of Roland's virtues, so instead, he returned to the hospital where he was first diagnosed the very next day. He was anxious to know what was happening to his body and if he had actually improved without realizing it. Simply, Roland was curious about his fate.

There was no grand sign other than the black ring to prove that his wish had actually been granted and he felt he had waited long enough for his luck to change. He felt he deserved better; the ring owed him that much for what it had taken from him. Though he was in no place to talk about debts, not after all the trouble he'd caused to everyone around him. Regardless, Roland still wanted to get some sort of sign, one that would allow him to return to living in ignorant bliss. Roland arrived barely after dawn; he wore a fine suit over his bandages. He looked like a rich mummy; he smelt like one, too- though his scent was heavy on the mummy and not all about the rich part of it. The first person to lay eyes on him paled as though they'd seen a ghost. Most medical staff have seen the most horrible conditions a man could suffer, yet hardly any of them had the stomach for Roland's repulsive being. It was so bad, in fact, that when Roland wasn't aware, a few doctors and Nurses took the day off. They decided it was best for their well-being and that they deserved it after coming in contact with Roland. They feared him like they feared the plague; if Roland could still cry, that would bring him to tears. Dejection had become a norm to him. He tried not to let their words get to him. He could hear them murmuring about him. There were a few who did attend to him. Roland felt moved by their kindness. He knew he didn't deserve any of it. Roland had become a very temperamental man. One minute he was the proudest man alive, and the very next, guilt would creep into his heart and cause him to crumble like the frail shadow of the man he truly was. He waited for a couple of hours before a doctor finally attended to him and afterwards, a few nurses came to attend to him. They were meticulous as they took off his bandages, each stripe of wool soaked in the black ooze and reeked of the horrid odor that plagued him, but rather than pain, he felt relief for the first time in months as they came off his body. It had been so long; Roland could hardly believe that it had only been a few months when it felt like he had spent his whole life in pain and bandages. For the first time in months, he received a long overdue bath and wipe away all the black ooze. There was plenty of disinfectants in his bathing water, so when he was done, he smelt more alcohol and menthol than pus and death. His eyes stung but compared to the pain; he was in just moments before he could bear the pain. Though his bandages were off they were far from done with him. Now that he was clean, they could see just how much damage his ailment had tolled on his body. They wanted to reschedule him for an operation. He had way too much dead skin and they were afraid they might even have to amputate. The doctor said he was to return in about a week after observing a strict diet to prepare him for the operation, but Roland refused. He insisted that it be done immediately and with the money he had, no one could tell him otherwise. In about an hour, he got his wish and had an operation carried out on him where they took off all his dead flesh. Luckily they didn't need to amputate anything, but the operation baffled the doctors. Roland wasn't too surprised; it was his wish- He wasn't going to die from being put under the knife. If only he was recovering just as well, then Roland would have nothing to complain about. Regardless, Roland was gladdened by the entire process. His operation was a success. He woke up a day later with relief despite the fact that he had risen with less skin than he had gone to bed with. Roland was simply glad to be alive and clean. He felt the operation was just what he needed to get his life back on track. Roland dared to glance at a mirror, and he didn't seem to care for how horrid his expressions had become. All he wanted to know was that he had survived. With his wealth, he was certain a couple million could replace all his old skin, maybe even remodel his face. He'd heard a lot about plastic surgery working miracles for models. There was no doubt in his mind that it could do the same for him. Roland was eager to be done with this tragic chapter of his tale and return to a better life, but sadly that wasn't the case.

Indeed, his operation's success was nothing short of a miracle. For the first time since his fame, Roland had made the headlines with the news of his condition turning heads and baffling the medical field all around the globe. Roland thought gendering attention would aid his improvement but his results far too mystified the doctors presiding over his case. To them, he had become a topic, something that needed to be studied. When he asked about the finer details when he grew too anxious to hold himself back, the doctor he consulted stared at him as though he was some alien discovery. He wasn't dying but he wasn't getting any better either. In fact, they all insisted that his condition hadn't taken a turn for better nor worse. Instead, it seemed to have paused. Roland wanted answers but not as much as they did. What was happening to him had never been recorded before. It was inhumane, to be honest. A breakthrough, some would call it. To be very frank with him, they revealed that he was very low on blood but showed no signs of ammonia; several of his vital organs had long failed, yet he went about as though he were perfectly normal, whereas a normal person would have either been put in a vegetative state or laid to rest. His heart rate was slowing to the point that anyone could have mistaken him for a walking corpse, his wounds weren't healing and through it, all Roland had only once complained of a mild headache since he arrived at the hospital. Every doctor in the building was horrified by how he was even alive, and the whole world wanted to know how a man could stand on his own two feet while his heart was barely pumping enough blood for his pulse to be taken. They tried to sugarcoat their reports, the last thing they wanted was for Roland to panic but even then, he could see it in their eyes. They eyed him with horror and those who weren't afraid of him had a glint in their eyes. Was it curiosity, intrigue, or sympathy- Roland didn't care for any of it? In the end, he was nothing to them; he was certain that they would put him under a knife to satisfy their urge to know what made him tick. It was just what the ring wanted, nothing more than to cause Roland despair. Roland wasn't going to allow himself to be toyed with that easily. He was outraged and distraught by all their words,

'Liars! All of you!' He railed and cried like a mad man as he rampaged through the hospital. They were going to sedate him, but Roland knew better. He was certain that the moment he was under, they would use his outburst as some excuse to examine him, an examination that would never end. He would become their 'lab rat'- Never! Roland could not allow himself to such a fate. He had given too much to dance in such a depressing tone. That was the only thing that plagued his mind as he fled from the hospital. He was a shadow of a man, but he still commanded great wealth and getting a scared taxi driver to follow his instructions was an easy task. As curious as they were about his condition, no one in the hospital really did put up a chase. The guards that could have easily seized him on his way out were too repulsed to actually confront him. Roland was glad to be getting away from the hospital, but he could still fill their eyes on him, even when they weren't really there. The way they all watched him when he fled. The way they stared at him with heavy eyes of reproach as though he was some unearthly creature. Staring at his own reflection churned his stomach and as he gritted his teeth, he could have sworn he heard laughing. The difference was that he wasn't afraid of it this time- it annoyed him.

Roland didn't like the way they watched him. When he arrived at the hotel, he didn't waste any time with the taxi driver or the receptionist. Hardly anyone could even look at him as he hurried into the elevator and went up to his suite. His room was clean, new sheets and all. It smelled a strong scent of roses and he found that they had even left sweets and drinks by his bed for him. It would have been a lovely welcome had his mood not already been ruined. He was like a candle with rage instead of fire. "Bagmeth !!!" He railed behind closed doors as he descended on the tray where the drinks and sweets they'd' left him were and tossed it all to the ground. There was a bottle of champagne waiting for him but seeing it only put a bitter taste in his mouth. He chucked the bottle across the room in a heartbeat and growled as he watched the bottle burst on a light post. "You have done it now! I've had enough of your bullshit!"

Roland was truly a man possessed as he tore through his room. Ripping the fine linen sheets of his bed, destroying the glorious chandelier that hung at the heart of the bedroom, ripping the head off a priceless statue that he once treasured and defacing paintings that people would have killed to have hanging in their galleries. Roland had descended into a blind rage, destroying any and everything within his reach. He did it as though all the things he destroyed were a part of Bagmeth and the dreadful ring on his finger. Seeing it repulsed him, he was afraid of having it taken from him but now he wanted nothing to do with it. "It's funny, right? You've had your laugh. Bastard! Bagmeth, come and take your damn ring! I'm done with it; I'm done with you! Now leave me the hell alone!"

His voice pierced the walls like razors and while he threw his fit, the lights began to flicker as cold air filled the room; he could tell right away that he had gotten its attention. He could feel the presence of the horrible entity he'd feared so dearly- watching him, mocking him. Roland could tell he wasn't alone, but not being able to see who he was mad at only made him angrier. "I know you're there! Are you afraid? Come take your fucking ring! I'm done!"

Roland was hysterical. He was revving for a fight; he didn't care if he was more bone than skin and muscle; he wanted to give Bagmeth a piece of his mind but no matter how loud his cries where Bagmeth wouldn't come to him. All he could feel was the entity's cold glare coming from nowhere and everywhere all at once. "You're not coming to me huh!" He spat when he had exhausted himself tearing his room apart and then he glanced down at his ring with an idea. If Bagmeth was not going to come to him, then he was going to summon the bastard the only other way he knew how. Roland turned his undivided attention to the ring. It looked like a horrid fit on him. Roland grimaced at how badly he had deteriorated. He blamed the ring on his finger for all his misfortunes. His hands were just as skinny and frail as the rest of his body. He used to wear gloves most of the time because he was too ashamed of how much of himself he had let go but now that he looked at them, he gritted his teeth in a fury. His hands were not easy on the eyes and then there was the rose diamond that stood out amongst his bony fingers. The ring's black gems seemed to bleed out evil with an almost alluring whisper persistently coming from them. Without the gem ever red glow, it had lost its charm. Instead, it felt as though the deeper he stared into them, the more alone he felt. Like the thousands of tormented souls wailing, trapped with the rose diamond Roland finally made sense of Donald's statement- 'the ring tried to eat me.' Donald was right. The pain from wearing the ring was no different from getting bitten. The horrible ring was like a vampire leeching off its latest victim, not letting go until it had drained them of every last drop of vitality within their veins. Roland felt like a fool. He was a fool. It took him far too long to realize it.

"You bastard! I've had enough of your games!" Roland roared with renewed determination as he hurried over to the side of his bed and found a letter opener. It was sharp with an aesthetic handle. He never used it but had it around simply for the lore it added to his room's décor. It was the closest thing to a blade he had in his room and that was just what he needed to follow through with the plan he had cooked up in his head. 'If Bagmeth is not going to take the ring from me, then the freaky-eyed man can just get his ring from the dumpster,' Roland thought defiantly. Since the ring had refused to leave his finger, 'The ring can keep the fucking thing!'

Without a second thought, he took the letter opener and pressed it at the base of his finger. Roland did not allow doubt to dissuade him as he forced it down below the ring and almost effortlessly, the steel clipped through bone and the finger came off without so much as a drop of blood being spilled. Roland was shocked at it. He almost didn't feel himself lose the finger. Roland stared at the wound on his pale palm and mused at the oddity of the situation but that didn't trouble him. The finger was off and so was the ring. He had nothing to worry about anymore; he was free. All he had to do now was get rid of the ring and then there would be no more nightmares, or the constant fear of being watched or the ever-present sense of impending doom that came with knowing Bagmeth would eventually appear to claim his price. Roland chuckled but then descended into hysterical laughter as he crumbled; his knees were weak. It felt as though a giant weight had been lifted off his shoulders as he sighed in relief. Roland was glad to be done with it all and a single finger felt like a fair enough trade, he sighed so deeply it felt as though all the air had flushed out his lungs but then he inhaled sharply as a chill ran down his spine. It was a dreadful sensation that he was far from estranged too. The relief he had just found was too short-lived to count as a victory now that a sensation far more sinister filled his room. The dreadful sense of death that had loomed over him for so long was now more dominant as he took the ring off. The weight he'd sworn was lifted off his body came down like a hammer on him. Sadly, it was more intent on crushing him this time. It was far worse than all the other times. When he felt it then, it was haunting but at least he could tell that whatever had an eye on him was merely toying with him but now he felt like his very soul was at great risk and there was nowhere to run to. Roland had only just realized how flawed his view of the whole picture was. He thought the ring was like a leash holding him down and with it gone, Bagmeth's rein would follow but he was wrong. He was less than a dog in Bagmeth's eyes; he was more like a fly- a slow one that had flew right into Bagmeth's palm and had been dancing there at Bagmeth's mercy. He thought that he'd always felt a cold gaze on his back but now that he could truly feel resentment glaring at him, he knew that had barely grasped the true meaning of the word despair. There was no doubt in Roland's mind that he had infuriated Bagmeth greatly. Roland felt like he had eyes on the back of his head, he could not see the creature, but he could feel it glaring into the depth of his dirty soul. Roland trembled as he felt piss roll down his leg and he fell short of breath. The lights that he had not smashed began to flicker and darkness crept so steadily across the room that even the light of day peering into the room curiously from the windows was muffled and turned grim. Roland trembled like he was naked on ice but then he gritted his teeth so hard he could taste blood on his tongue. 'Enough of this bullshit!' With new vigor and fire in his eyes, Roland thought defiantly, 'I don't have the ring on me anymore.' That was right; the ring was no longer latched on to his body, Bagmeth had no right over him- those were the rules, weren't they? Telling himself those words, he gathered the courage and strength to get back on his feet and take a bold stand for himself. He wasn't going to beg for his life, he felt like he was in control and for that, he was willing to give the presence trying to bully him a piece of his mind.

"Fucking leave me alone! I'm done with your ring, and I'm done with you!" Roland yelled at the top of his lungs as he spun about the room, daring the entity to confront him face to face. Come to think of it. He'd never seen anything other than its eyes. Its voice was dreadful but so were the barks from a small dog. In fact, if the entity was so shy, then its bark must have been worse than its bite. The more he thought about it, the more confident he grew; he was half convinced that his fear was unwarranted. It was all in his head. For all he knew, the entity might not have been as scary as he thought it was, but just as he had that train of thought, he turned to regret his words as he came face to face with the most ungodly creature on the face of the earth.

He only caught a glimpse; the eyes that he thought were scary afar were now a hair's breadth away from his. They were the most beautiful jewels he'd ever laid eyes on; the blue was infinitely calm and alluring like an abyss with no end, whereas the red eye was a fire that threatened to swallow him whole. It was beautiful but it would have seized him without hesitation. The beauty of its eyes contrasted the horror that was its being. The entity was something he could not put into words but if he was forced to, he would sum its existence up in a simple phrase; 'It was a greedy death'. Roland hid his face but just as he did, he saw blood pool at his feet. His mind could not bear the creature's sight, and it took a toll on his body. His eyes were bloodshot, and his nose began to bleed as a wild wind blew through the room, knocking things off the wall and slamming him into the door behind him as though he weighed less than a feather. Roland forced his eyes shut; he was too afraid of what would happen if he allowed himself to see it again. He felt that if he made eye contact any longer than he already had, then surely he would die. Roland could hear the walls creak as though something large was ripping through them. The floor shook as his large bed was flung across the room, a small stool crashed into the door an inch away from his way, causing him to flinch and shrink. Roland muttered in utter terror, trembling like a lost child. He knew he was at its mercy and was sure that it was only a matter of time before its wrath would descend on him. He felt a pressure mount on his neck; he could feel it squeezing the life out of him as it lifted him up into the air. Roland choked and groaned as he felt its warm breath on its face. He was afraid that if he dared to open his eyes, he'd find his head between two large rows of flesh-rendering teeth, so he kept his eyes shut. It growled over him, and Roland knew that there was no escape, but when all hope was lost, there was a knock on the door behind him.

He could hear the entity's frustration as it dropped him with a loud thud and just as suddenly as its evil presence filled the room, it vanished, leaving Roland panting in his own piss and sweat. When he opened his eyes, blood trickled down the side of one of them. His room had seen better days but now it was totaled beyond recognition. No one would believe the room and all the décor within it once cost at least several thousand dollars to rent a night. The furniture and bed aside, the windows were smashed wide open. It was just as though the creature had fled through and the sheer size of its mass had destroyed them, but Roland hadn't heard when they were smashed, neither had he heard the knocking on the door behind him. His eardrums had burst and were ringing. The little he could still hear was muffled and almost incomprehensible. He was confused. Roland did not allow himself to entertain the delusion of safety in the entity's hasty retreat. 'Why didn't it finish me off?' As he caressed the mark its large phalanges had left on his neck, he thought. Roland didn't want to die but if he'd learnt anything from his short time with the ring was that Bagmeth didn't act without reason, if he was still alive then Bagmeth had more in store for him and that scared him far more than the thought of death. The incessant knocking on the door wouldn't stop until it finally got to Roland's hearing.

"Are you okay in there Mr. Butler?" A voice called. Roland didn't notice it at first but when he listened closer, he thought there was something familiar about it. He was sure he'd heard it somewhere; he just couldn't tell whose voice it was. He reached for the door and found himself shaking both his hands- his entire body was jittery. He couldn't help it; he was still shaken up by his quick brush with death. Roland pressed his ear against the door with nervous pants as he hesitantly held the doorknob. "Whose asking?" He replied; he couldn't tell if his voice was a whisper or a yell but getting a reply was proof that it had gotten through to them on the other side.

"It's Detective Beckham. We've met before. I'm not sure if you remember." The familiar voice replied. Roland remembered the detective; how could he forget him? Roland let out a sigh as he opened the door and just as the voice had said, there in his doorway stood Detective Beckham standing in the hotel's hallway with two other police officers poised readily by his side. They seemed to recoil at him, but Detective Beckham was different, he didn't so much as flinch at Roland's distorted sight neither did his expression betrayed his surprise. He was unfazed and unreadable, acting as though Roland hadn't aged a day in months and oddly, Roland found himself somewhat relieved by the Detective's demeanor. Unlike how the rest of the world looked at him as though he was some sort of dirty thing.

"I remember you…" Roland leered at the man as he glanced at the other officers in his way, "I'm fine. Now leave me alone-" Being alone was the last thing Roland wanted but being in the company of a detective and some men in uniform was the last thing he wanted, especially knowing what he'd done. He was afraid of being alone. He was afraid 'It' would come back to finish him off but the men before him were not the kind of company he wanted. He tried to retreat but Beckham stopped him. "The hell do you want?"

"We just want to have a little chat with you-" Beckham replied, his expression was just as hard to read as the first time they'd met. His voice was calm, alarmingly so. Beckham sounded like a parent trying to get a confession out of mischievous little boy, it was almost condescending and his eyes unnerved Roland. Roland had no interest in talking to the man, not while he was still shaken up. He wanted to at least calm himself down or he was sure he'd be all over the place and crack under Beckham's probing. He feared the man's skill just as much as he feared death; he knew he couldn't hide anything from the detective if he tried.

"Well, I am not feeling chatty; I've had a rough day, so if you'd excuse me." Roland snapped as he tried to slam the door shut in their face, but the door wouldn't budge. He hadn't the strength to move it against Beckham's might as he stepped in the way and shoved it back with him along with. Beckham said something and flashed a warrant as he and his men allowed themselves into the room. Roland wished they hadn't. It was the worst possible time for him to be having guests. 'What is that God awful stench...' one of the officers scowled with a hand over his face as Roland bowed his head in a bitter disgrace. Both the officers seemed very irritated by it all. Even the unflinching Beckham scrunched his nose. Roland couldn't blame them. The scent of roses that had welcomed him was gone and it wasn't his piss that stunk the room up. It was the smell the rose diamond had cursed him with. The pungent ever-present stench of death itself that had clung to him. They were all startled and also surprised by how torn up Roland's room was, but not Beckham, though.

Beckham's thought process was very different from those of his colleagues, he didn't look all too surprised but when he glanced at Roland there was confusion in his eyes. There was no doubt in Roland that the detective suspected that he wasn't the one that had torn the room apart so thoroughly. He was too frail to have the strength for such a feat, but the detective kept all his thoughts to himself while he examined the room. Another thing Roland noted about the detective was his composure; it was strong and gave the impression that he'd seen worse.

"Sir! You got to see this..." One of the officers called to Beckham with a grim expression on his face, he sounded shaken by something he'd found on the floor and Beckham rushed to him just as the man called. All Roland could do was follow them with his eyes while the other officer loomed over him; it was obvious the officer was standing guard just in case he tried to flee- not that he had the strength nor will to do so if the chance even presented itself to him. The officer had every right to be shaken, he'd found something disturbing. He'd found a finger lying on the floor alongside some rubble from the wrecked furniture.

Roland paled at the sight.

"My finger..." He gasped to all their surprise. They stared at him as though he were deranged but then Beckham noticed something off about him. Roland's expressions marbled the Detective greatly. He could hardly ever tell if Roland was putting up a farce or if he was genuinely in shock at the discovery.

"Care to explain?" Detective Beckham asked. He felt it was too early to jump to any conclusions. Regardless of how bad everything looked.  "While you're at it, care to tell me all about your visit to Mr. Donald Sutton's place while you're at it."

His words didn't reach Roland. The world seemed to be spinning. Roland shook his head with his eyes beading as he tried to desperately crawl away from them. The second officer grabbed hold of him but then he began to flail wildly in hysteria staring at his hand in utter terror. Roland was so afraid it unnerved the men around him. None of them had a clue of what had set him off or what he saw that made him so afraid he could barely even utter a proper sentence. Roland had not registered that the police were about to arrest him regardless of his outburst, and he was in too much of a panic to acknowledge the world around him. Roland was so numb from fear that he hadn't felt its bite, nor could he recall when it happened. All he knew was that he was more afraid of the ring that had returned to a finger on his hand when he was sure he had cut it off just moments ago.

# CHAPTER
## NINE

From the outside, it looked cheerless, rough, and cold. Sandstone bricks and marble pillars made up most of the building's outer structure. It was difficult to see through its curtained windows, but the uncomfortable atmosphere from within it could be felt outside. The was a peculiar hard wooden door at its entrance; the bartender was reading a newspaper and wasn't exactly welcoming but yet Roland had managed to get himself a drink and sat at the furthest corner from all the other customers. He wanted to be alone as his eyes surveyed the establishment like a fox that had strayed too far from its den. No one had acknowledged his presence. It was as dire inside as it was on the outside. Stone beams supported the upper floor and a large, brightly lit chandelier provided illumination for the whole place. The walls were decorated with hunting trophies, from stuffed raccoons to deer, but it looked like it hadn't been cleaned in years. The pub itself was weird. It had contrasting themes, but he felt that was what drew people to it, its unique style and charm. The few people inside were silent and kept to themselves, but regardless of whoever they were, Roland hoped they'd continue to leave him just as he was leaving them alone. He seemed out of place; it wasn't his regular joint. In fact, nothing about the place rang a bell to him. He could not even remember when or how he'd gotten there, to begin with. There was a query on his face, and he was just about to step out for some fresh air and to arrange his thoughts when the last person he wanted to see was at his table.

"How's my favorite ring bearer faring?" Bagmeth cheered with open arms as he joined Roland at his table. Bagmeth was as grandiose as ever, from his hair to the outstanding fabric of his suit. He seemed rather excited to see Roland, but the feeling was not mutual and instead, he received a glare from a resentful Roland. The hate in his eyes was pointed solely at the pompous man who joined him nonchalantly for a drink, but Bagmeth didn't seem to care for his hostility. "I've met a lot of men in my time, but you're one of the few who has lasted this long. You should be proud."

Roland decided to ignore him. He had more important things to attend to, like the roast pork he was served and the fine lady that had joined him and was gently caressing his hair while he ate. He hadn't the time of day for Bagmeth and imply implored the strange man to leave him alone. "Why the cold shoulder, Roland?" Bagmeth chuckled, "Are you still mad about the finger?"

"Screw you Bagmeth!" Roland hissed, "I've made all my wishes. I'm done with you and your bullshit! So, you can take your ring and fuck off."

Bagmeth smirked and leaned closer to Roland; he seemed bigger all of a sudden. It wasn't the way he poised himself but rather as though the table itself had shrunk and Roland along with it. He took a fork from the tray beside him and decided to help himself to some of Roland's pork. Roland was sour at the action but was still rather confident that Bagmeth wouldn't want to cause a scene in such a crowded place. He leered at the man as he chewed with relish and smiled back at him.

"You're right. Rules are rules. I'll take the ring back." Bagmeth grinned over a mouth full of pork. Then he helped himself to some wine that just conveniently seemed to be waiting by him. "I hope you enjoy your immortality, but let's get one thing straight: You're not done with me. I say when we're done."

"Why do you care?" Roland grimaced and Bagmeth made a face. Rather than feigning annoyance like he was doing just prior, Bagmeth's mood had done a 180. The look on his face was like a smirk. His bright bewitching eyes had a wicked glint in them as his lips suddenly stretched further than his cheeks, touching his ears in the most ungodly visage. He looked gleeful, handsome, and monstrous all at once. "My god-"

"It's too late for God to hear you now Roland. You see… I've done this a thousand times. I've met your kind, and you're all the same. Vain, naïve, greedy, selfish… all the best qualities of a good prey. Yet no matter how many of you I meet, I'll never get used to a foul mouth.

Honestly, I can tolerate a lot of things, but I don't like being insulted." Bagmeth growled. "Especially not from a low life like you. I feel I need to discipline you."

Roland paled and shrank in his seat.

"Everyone's watching; you don't want to cause a scene, do you?" Roland sputtered nervously as Bagmeth laughed. How was any of this possible? Roland's mind was in a fit when he glanced about the pub hoping someone would at least notice what was going on, but the place was deserted. There wasn't even a bartender behind the counter. They were all alone. When Bagmeth laughed, it was the same horrid laugh from his nightmares that had always haunted him both conscious and unconscious, the sign that he was always being watched. He was only just realizing that Bagmeth did not work for the monster from his nightmares- it was Bagmeth all along.

'Who is watching?' Bagmeth's ungodly voice seemed to call from all directions. Suddenly the place felt smaller. Somehow, Bagmeth had managed to empty the pub- 'Pub? What pub? - Where am I?'

Bagmeth laughed hysterically as his eyes peered deeply into Roland's thoughts.

"Took you long enough. Glad to see you're waking up. This wouldn't be any fun without you awake..." Bagmeth chuckled as he leaned over for some more pork but rather than roast pork being in the tray in front of them, what laid was a roast human corpse. 'Long pork,' Bagmeth called it with a grin as he thrust his fork into the intestines of the corpse in the tray before them and ate as though it were the best meal he'd had in years.

Roland gagged and gasped as he threw his fork away at the sight of the human corpse and blood where pork and wine should have been. None of anything happening made any sense; he wanted it all to end but Bagmeth ate with a ravenous appetite and ignored him; with every passing second, his guise of humanity slipped away, revealing just how much of a demon he truly was. His large jaw shifted to reveal rows of razor-sharp teeth as he chuckled with delight and gnawed on human bone like it were a common treat to him.

"What's the matter, dear?" The woman by his side cooed, "You're not eating anymore? I thought Marcus was delicious-". The voice, he recognized it before he had even dared to face her. As he looked up to see that the lady he was with all along was his late wife, Helen, or what was left of her, at least. Where its eyes were supposed to be, were hollow and black, with most of its skin left reduced to char and bone. It leaned in to kiss him and in fear, Roland shoved it to the ground watching in disdain as she fell apart.

"Tsk Tsk! That's not very nice Roland, no way to treat a lady at all," Bagmeth smirked with an off-putting mouth full of meat as he spoke, "Oh my, you truly are scum,"

"Where am I! what are you doing to me?" Roland cried but Bagmeth didn't respond. He was too busy gnawing on the fingers of the meal set in front of them. "I followed the rules. I made all my wishes; what more do you want from me? Take the fucking ring and leave me the hell alone! Let me live my life in peace,"

"Live? Funny that you would say that," Bagmeth snickered, "I doubt you've noticed, but you're already a corpse- you just can't die."

Roland's eyes betrayed his surprise and that put a smile on Bagmeth's face.

"You didn't realize? That's rich! HA!" Bagmeth laughed; it was the first time his ever-calm demeanor could not mask his malicious intent, "In that case, I guess I'll have to discipline you later, for now- I'll enjoy the show."

HIS WORDS WERE HEAVY AND FOREBODING. ROLAND WATCHED as Bagmeth declared his intent gallantly and then disappeared into the dark as slowly as a passing fog. In his absence, the reality that Roland had come through to find himself seemed no longer able to maintain itself and slowly, the darkness about what once appeared to be a pub began to consume the dream that never was. Roland was in a panic. He had nowhere to run but was desperate to flee from the darkness. He was afraid of what it would do to him. He had yet to realize that it wasn't the fear of what it would do to him that he fled from so desperately but the fear of returning to what it had already done to him. In his dream like state, he had almost forgotten how cruel reality really was. When the darkness swept over him, not only did it consume the dream that he mistook for reality, but it also took the façade of normality that he was deceived by. It reminded him of what he really looked like; it was Bagmeth's delight to remind him of just how far gone he was. His skin was the first to go as pores began to spread across his body, consuming his flesh and causing what was left to fall off into oblivion, leaving a scarred, rotting body in its wake. Roland screamed and cried as he felt the skin of his face wither away with his eyelids along with it but that was merely the beginning of his horrors. When he tried to calm himself down, he glanced down at his palms and saw as his fingers began to snap and point in the wrong direction, he felt like he was in hell and all the while, Bagmeth laughed from the void.

A BRIGHT LIGHT STUNG HIS EYES WHEN HE WOKE UP GROGGILY to find himself in some sort of cell. There were no steel bars, and it was more of a room, but Roland could tell at first glance that it was a cell meant to confine him. The walls of his cell were padded with foam, and there was a faint scent in the air. Roland couldn't quite tell what it was, but he was at least glad to awaken to something other than the stench that always clung to him. The air about the cell was serene compared to how hectic the past few days of his life had been. When Roland came to, he found himself squinting. He could barely move, then he found himself bound in a straitjacket. 'Where am I?' Roland thought groggily as he rolled over and managed to get himself into an upright position so he could glance about the confines of his small cell. He learnt that he was in a psych ward for the criminally insane. He had trouble moving around, but a few officers rushed in to gag him the moment he did. They were afraid he was going to try at biting his tongue off. The state he was in when they restrained him led them all to believe that he was suicidal and that was why he was placed under suicide watch. Everyone insisted that he was criminally insane. It took him a while but with time, he learnt that the driver that had taken him to Donald's house wasn't as loyal as Roland thought he was. Though in all honesty, Roland couldn't bring himself to blame the man. While Roland was taken into custody, the young driver went to the police and testified against him. Roland had no chance of convincing them that he wasn't a mad man. Finding his finger lying nonchalantly on the ground at his suite led them to believe he had been mutilating himself for the longest time. His outburst at the hospital was also recorded against him. They had more than enough evidence to convict him of Donald's murder too, but Roland never made it to a court.

THE DOCTORS THAT HAD ATTENDED TO HIM CONCLUDED HE was neither in the right state of mind or of good enough health to make an appearance in a hospital. Some people would say he was lucky to have escaped appearing before a judge; surely, the heinous nature of his crime would have gotten him a life sentence. Roland didn't care what they thought; calling him lucky didn't make him feel any less perplexed by it all. His encounter, Bagmeth's words… he couldn't get them out of his head. To make matters worse, he couldn't sleep longer than half an hour anymore. It wasn't because of the nightmares he used to have. He hadn't had another nightmare in days, not ever since the nightmare where he saw Bagmeth. When he did fall asleep, he'd wake back up in start feeling more exhausted than before he'd even tried to get some shut-eye. It was like his brain was always snapping him back to reality before he could actually get any rest; maybe it was because he was too afraid Bagmeth would return to him in his dreams. Roland felt vulnerable and as the last of his strength drained from his broken body, he became a distorted replication of the man he used to be just months ago. Sleep deprived and scared, Roland was convinced his brain was slowly devouring itself in fear. At times he would hallucinate; he would feel as though something was lurking in the shadows and then he would let out blood-curdling cries until a guard or two was forced to come in to check on him. Though they wouldn't believe it, most of the time, his hallucinations were not symptoms of his madness. They were very real like the cursed ring that he still wore. At times he would be so out of control that the attendants would be forced to use more drastic approaches to calm him. He'd gotten sedated a few times but even then, he was far from docile. It became a fact that no matter how high the dose he was administered, it never kept him under longer than a few minutes. His medications were more than enough to knock an elephant on its ass and yet they did nothing for him. Not even the painkillers that he sought could save him from his agony. The pain that he constantly endured from his sore body was hellish and Roland was repulsed by his own stench.

ROLAND'S LIFE HAD BECOME A VICIOUS DULL CYCLE OF waking up to tasteless meals, bright lights, voices, and drugs. It was bleak and was by far the worse point in his life compared to all the hell he'd been through over the course of the past few months. In his confinement's first days, Roland would lie motionless in his cell like a dead log. There was nothing he could do with his hands restrained, so he submitted to his maddening state. But there was a silver lining, though a very small one at that. It was the fact that he was allowed to have visitors. Despite his notorious case, Roland was not surprised to see that not a single journalist had dared to visit him in his cell. Most would assume they were all too afraid of him to put themselves alone in a room with him, but Roland knew better. It was the same with his wealth. It didn't matter how much dust he raised or how scandalous his existence was- the ring would not allow anyone to remember him. It was all part of his whole personal torment. Though there was one exception. Detective Beckham had not forgotten him. In the earlier weeks of his incarceration, the Detective paid several visits to his cell and was practically the only other human being he'd spoken to. The Detective's visits were a godsend to Roland, but it was too apparent that the Detective was not always coming back at leisure or merely because he was fond of Roland or anything of that nature. He had a goal he intended to achieve and despite knowing that Roland went out of his way to stall the man, he knew that so long as the Detective did not reach his objective, he was bound to return for another conversation. Beckham always had a long face on during his visits, and Roland knew why but he didn't care. Despite all he'd gone through, he was still a selfish man at heart- there was no changing that.

BECKHAM HAD ALWAYS BEEN DIFFERENT FROM EVERYONE ELSE in Roland's eyes. No one looked at him as though he was still human, no one other than the Detective. Beckham could smell a rat. He seemed to be the only one who found Roland's tale to be loose at the ends. Roland wondered how he'd been allowed into the cell with a ring. It was a feat he doubted anyone could manage. As time went on, he realized that no one could see it anymore, he tried to trick one of the guards into taking it from him, but they stared at his fingers and saw nothing there. Everyone thought it was merely part of his delusions. Bagmeth wasn't a fool. He had no intention of letting Roland off that easily. The ring was bound to him and him alone, and it was going to remain that way until Bagmeth was '...done with him.' Roland couldn't give a ring away even if he wanted to, but he knew that so long as he had the ring- Bagmeth would return for him.

Detective Beckham had had his eye on Roland for the longest time. He thought having Roland confined to a single space would be a good step towards achieving his goals but even then, his investigations turned up fruitless. He wanted to solve the mystery that revolved around Roland and tie a knot to all the loose ends. He was certain that Roland was connected to a lot more than just Donald's murder, like the deaths of his boss, family, and wife's lover. Detective Roland was so driven to find answers that many would have thought the case was personal to him. Roland couldn't tell if the Detective's conviction was out of resentment or a strong sense of justice, but in the end, he was gladdened to have contact with another human being every now and then. It was the only thing that made his hell bearable. The isolation was eating at him, literally. Roland was losing skin like a dog shedding hair; his condition was only worsening and there was no medication that could reverse it. Though Detective Beckham never spoke up about his curiosity, he always wondered how Roland had essentially lost everything he lived for overnight and then rose to a height that many envied, only to topple back down again in the short span of months. Any time he tried to talk about it. Roland would become defensive or straight-up unresponsive. Roland had fear in his eyes and spent most of the time trying to stir up the small talk as though the two were old friends. It was annoying to Beckham. What annoyed Beckham the most was that all his investigations led to dead ends. When he tried to look into the source of Roland's money, he found that they came from accounts that couldn't be traced and when he tried to investigate the cause of the fire at Roland's home, he found nothing incriminating but that also gave the impression that the fire simply erupted from thin air. None of it made any sense to him and none of it ever would because he knew nothing about the ring. Roland could see the man's stress, but he never said a word about it. Eventually, the Detective had enough of Roland's ploy and finally decided to close his book on the entire investigation. He figured it was about time he let the case go and so he did.

WHEN BECKHAM FINALLY THREW IN THE TOWEL THAT marked the end of his visits, it was then that Roland truly despaired. The mental hospital he had been put in was no better than a prison yard; the difference was that the sun would have touched his face at least in a prison yard. Roland found himself muzzled one day. He was held among the worst cases in the states, yet they treated him like he was the unsightliest patient. He was under isolation and the only time he saw another human being was when one came into his cell to feed him- when they did go out of their way to ensure he ate, that was. It was like he was never in their care. They claimed to have him under a suicide watch, yet they didn't care if he lived or died. He barely had the strength to stand on his own two feet. Having the ring clinging to him only made Roland feel more afraid of life itself. Roland's life was bleak and stressful. It was so stressful that, at times, Roland began to believe that he truly had lost his mind. Maybe that would have been better for him. If he were insane, then maybe reality wouldn't hurt as badly as it did. He hardly ate. Over time all the teeth in his mouth had fallen out, so he gave up on trying. Most of the attendants who brought his meals were too disgusted by his appearance to bother feeding him. At times he would grovel over his food like a maggot, then he lost his sense of hunger all together and simply left whatever they brought to him to go bad. Other times he was too weak to even budge was the corner of his cell where he balled himself up. With time Roland forgot what it felt like to be free. Could the life he even lived count as a free one? He was at the ring's mercy when he wasn't slaving away at a desk for his snobbish boss. Though he never truly surrendered himself to the oblivion that awaited him, he was too tired to care about not dying anymore. He knew Bagmeth was coming for him at some point and deep down, he was looking forward to seeing his own finale. Roland begged for death.

His sleepless nights left him with dreadful hallucinations and splitting headaches. The death that he was so afraid of, he now yearned for. 'Anything to escape reality one last time,' He thought in the corner of his cell one evening when he finally managed to close his eyes and fell asleep for the first time in months.

WHEN A MAN GOES TOO LONG WITHOUT ANY SHUT-EYE, HIS brain begins to deteriorate, and without a brain to tell the heart and all the other important organs what to do, such a man is good as dead. For better or worse, Roland was the kind of man that could not die. He was so exhausted from all the starvation and sleep deprivation that when he finally did sleep, he slept like a literal corpse. Roland was out for days. It was the best nap he'd had in years; little did he know that he was pronounced dead while he slept. Roland didn't have a pulse or a heartbeat he hadn't had one in a month since his last wish. He was in constant pain, yet while he slept, he was absolutely numb. His body was of no value to the psych ward; naturally, they would have had him incinerated. His tragic tale would have finally come to an end- Bagmeth felt that would have been too merciful. Instead, he took Roland and was more than eager to welcome him on. He finally woke to find himself in the casket Bagmeth had picked for him. It was a crude-looking thing made from black wood. It was the kind of casket the dead would not be able to rest easy in. Roland stirred from his blissful slumber to a familiar laugh, a laugh that made his soul tremble. He opened his eyes and there Bagmeth stood, smirking down at him. He was wearing a fine suit with gloves to go with it and a top hat that he held to his chest like an apologetic Victorian-aged gentleman. Roland could barely move his neck; he was too cramped where he laid and then he saw Bagmeth speak.

"It was a real fun run, wasn't it, Mr. Butler?" Bagmeth said. His smile was just as charming as it was cruel. A true devil.

"Where am I?" Roland panicked, he couldn't feel his legs and his fingers wouldn't budge. All he could see was the roof of a wooden coffin and Bagmeth peering down at him. The stench of death was so strong it stung his eyes. His hands were stiff as concrete, but it wasn't just his hands. His whole body wouldn't listen to him, no matter how hard he tried to move. The only part of his body he could move was his eyes. Bagmeth didn't seem to care. He was just his ever so cheerful self.

"Where are we? Ha! Your funeral, silly…" Bagmeth replied with a taunting laugh, "But don't worry, it's just me. No one was going to claim your body, not after how horrible a person you were. So, I figured it was about time I got my ring back,"

"My funeral! That's not possible… I'm not dead," Roland retorted. "Not yet as! - Not ever…"

'I wished for it,' Roland thought but then his eyes betrayed his revelation. He had been too naïve; the wishes were never in his favor. His soul had always been

Bagmeth's prize from the moment the foul creature laid eyes on him at the bar. Roland was only just realizing that as Bagmeth's red eye seemed to glisten brighter than usual. Bagmeth was not a man. He was a demon and Roland had been dancing in his palm the entire time. An utter fool to his own greed.

"Sure… You might still be alive but sadly, I can't say the same for that poor shell of yours. Your body is dead and rotting, my friend. It's best to put you in the ground before people start to ask questions about the walking corpse," Bagmeth replied in jest. Bagmeth made the whole transaction seem like a game; honestly, he saw it as one. Betting on how long it would take a ring bearer to destroy themselves, then he smirked again at the thought. Roland didn't know what to expect as he watched Bagmeth reach over him for his hand. Bagmeth seemed fixated on the finger his ring was on. "I'll be needing this."

ROLAND WAS ALREADY PALER THAN A GHOST. FROM THE smirk, he could almost tell what Bagmeth had in mind to do to him, and he tried to cry and protest. If Bagmeth had a better nature, Roland was more than desperate to appeal to it but all he could do was watch dejectedly as Bagmeth slowly broke his finger from his hand and pulled it off like it was a dead branch still clinging to an old tree. Bagmeth had gleefully retrieved his ring and then stuffed the finger he'd taken from Roland into his suit's pocket like it was a sort of trophy he had just earned. It was a joyous occasion for the demon, and it leered as he saw tears roll down Roland's cheeks. Roland was at a loss for words as he stared up at Bagmeth in sheer terror. "Rigor mortis can be a bitch don't you say… Ha!"

"PLEASE… DON'T HURT M-" ROLAND TRIED TO PLEAD WITH Bagmeth but while he spoke, Bagmeth reached into his mouth and grabbed his tongue, interrupting him. Bagmeth's nails felt like pincers attached to a clamp. 'You're hurting me,' Roland tried to cry but could barely mouth the words with his tongue out, even if he could have spoken clearly. Bagmeth didn't care about his pain. Bagmeth was enjoying himself, relishing in the pain that Roland went through. He'd wanted to do this to the man for the past month but every time he confronted Roland, he ended up sparing him. He knew the longer Roland suffered. The more satisfying his demise would be.

"You're a foul-mouthed man Mr. Butler," Bagmeth said as his eyes lit up devilishly, he was going to enjoy every bit of what he had in store for Roland. "I did say I'd punish you."

"Nuh- No…" Roland tried to protest but he couldn't form the words with his tongue being held out with a vice-like grip and all he could do was grunt and plead with his eyes, but Bagmeth was never going to buy into his desperation. Instead, Bagmeth casually pulled his tongue from his mouth, laughing as he watched the muscles rip and give way before he threw it on the floor with a grimace like it was something filthy. In his words, it was longer than he thought.

ROLAND WAS IN SHOCK, CHOKING ON HIS OWN BLOOD. HE wanted to scream but he couldn't. All his attempts came out as blood-curdling gurgles and coughs. Bagmeth then forced the roof of the casket down and while Roland tried to cry and put up a fight, he could hear the cruel devil slowly sealing his casket shut with loud bangs as he drove nails into the casket's sides. Once he was done, he began to drag Roland to a grave he'd prepared. Roland could feel himself being dragged. He could even hear Bagmeth humming an odd tone as he did so and lowered the casket into the earth. First, there was the sound of gravel and dirt falling into the casket, some of which even got into the casket, and soon after, Roland could hear the silence of the earth. Roland felt he was being buried alive, but in the state he was in, could he truly be considered 'Alive?'

THE DARKNESS ENCASED HIM; ROLAND KNEW THERE WAS NO escaping. He was going to rot down there. The immortality that he sort was more of a curse than a wish. For the eternity that would follow, all he had were his thoughts and the knowing feeling that Bagmeth was still watching him from beyond. Roland regretted so much in his life and cried until his eyes shriveled him and he looked like a proper corpse, but even then, there was no taking back his wishes.

BAGMETH HAD GOTTEN HIS FILL OFF ROLAND BUTLER'S escapades and with the Rose Diamond within his possession again. He felt it was about time he found a new bearer for his precious ring.

www.ingramcontent.com/pod-product-compliance
Lightning Source LLC
Chambersburg PA
CBHW071155300726
48975CB00004B/1164